Praise for Susan Hatler's Work

"Susan always provides readers with a quick romantic getaway with these Date books."
— *Getting Your Read On*

"If you're looking for a fun, light read then look no further!"
— *Night Owl Reviews*

"I was laughing and smiling throughout the story."
— *Tifferz Book Review*

"I can't get enough of this series!!!"
— *Books Are Sanity!!!*

"Susan Hatler's books make me laugh out loud while also touching my heart."
— *Virna DePaul, New York Times Bestselling Author*

Titles by Susan Hatler

An Unexpected Date

Better Date than Never Series

Love at First Date (Book 1)
Truth or Date (Book 2)
My Last Blind Date (Book 3)
Save the Date (Book 4)
A Twist of Date (Book 5)
License to Date (Book 6)
Driven to Date (Book 7)
Up to Date (Book 8)
Déjà Date (Book 9)
Date and Dash (Book 10)

Teen Novels

Shaken
See Me

Déjà Date

(Better Date than Never #9)

Susan Hatler

Déjà Date
Copyright © 2015 by Susan Hatler

ISBN-13: 978-1508553946
ISBN-10: 1508553947

Cover Design by Elaina Lee, For The Muse Design
www.forthemusedesign.com

Chapter One

I was an ugly duckling who turned into a swan, and I can't decide which was worse. Yeah, I may have had to endure the nickname "Marshmallow Melinda" all through elementary school but at least I had gotten to indulge in the world's most scrumptious creation: the chocolate marshmallow fudge bars from Bernie's Bakery.

I wanted one *now*.

As I pushed open the yellow shabby-chic door of Bernie's Bakery in East Sacramento, the *ding-a-ling* of a bell chimed overhead. I stepped inside. Although it had been almost two months since my last visit, the familiar warmth washed over me as I inhaled the sweet scents of banana bread, carrot cake, and something that smelled suspiciously like sourdough. Bernie's Bakery had always been a home away from home for me, and I would've smiled if my situation weren't so dire.

My heels clicked along the wooden floor as I strode to the back of the very long line of Monday morning patrons, who were waiting to order their espresso drinks and delicious pastries from this popular bakery.

For over a decade, I've forced myself to opt for Bernie's bran muffins instead of those fudge bars my taste buds really craved. But that was about to change, because I'd never been so stressed in my life. Tension mounted inside me as my gaze flicked to the chocolate marshmallow fudge bars lined up behind the glass display case. Three left. One was mine. All mine.

I licked my bottom lip.

Changing my diet to ditch the nickname "Marshmallow Melinda" hadn't been easy, and my willpower had held strong even when I'd worked here part-time through college. But where had being size four gotten me anyway?

I'm a twenty-seven-year-old customer service representative who was recently laid off from my job of four years, forcing me to move in with a roommate to save on expenses. Goodbye independence, hello lint remover—my roommate, Ginger, had two kittens, and feline hair was so *not* my friend.

Yeah, I'd hated my career—listening to people's complaints day in and day out wasn't exactly a mood booster. But at least it had paid well. I couldn't say the same about the menial temp jobs available. All my spare time in the past seven weeks had been consumed with sending out résumés and going on interviews. I hadn't even had a chance to visit my mother let alone come in to say hi to Bernie at his bakery, which was in the same neighborhood where my mom lived.

I also still hadn't found a new job. As such, my bank account was dry. Since my mom had called last night to invite me over for a visit, this was my final stop on the way to her place—a gorgeous house in the historic Fabulous Forties neighborhood—where I'd have the utter humiliation of asking to dip into the inheritance I swore I'd never touch.

I'd truly reached rock bottom. Thus, my need for the chocolate marshmallow fudge bar in order to offset my misery. I glanced nervously at my watch, keenly aware that I had to act fast before my roommate's sister, Mary Ann, arrived.

In an effort to cheer me up last night, Mary Ann— who I didn't even know very well—had treated me to an expensive dinner at a trendy restaurant, which was very generous of her. Unfortunately, I found myself wishing I'd brought earplugs. Steamed lobster with a buttery Chardonnay? Good. Incessant gripes about her alcoholic father who was in rehab? Bad.

Couldn't she appreciate that she still *had* a dad? Mine had gone and died on me during a freak hot air balloon accident when I was fourteen. And taking any of the life insurance money resulting from his death felt wrong. But I was desperate.

To top everything off, Mary Ann had swung by the condo this morning to give her final reimbursement check to her sister—apparently Mary Ann had owed Ginger a hefty sum of money—and had invited herself to meet me at Bernie's Bakery. Before I had time to protest, she'd zipped out the door saying she'd see me there in fifteen minutes.

First, I didn't want Mary Ann or her sister (aka: my landlord) to know I was broke. And second, I didn't need anyone witnessing my final moment of defeat when I chowed down that fudge bar.

I'd worked hard to project a good image and I would not have my cover blown now. My perfect persona was currently a complete façade, but nobody needed to know that. Maybe if the line moved fast enough, I could scarf down that alluring fudge bar before she arrived. Now that sounded like a good plan.

My heart pounded in my chest as I moved up in line and my mouth watered just thinking about that sweet chocolate melting on my tongue. How I'd survived thirteen years without eating one of those fudge bars was beyond me. Two more patrons ahead of me then that delicious treat would be *mine*. As I stared at the row of decadent delights, the *ding-a-ling* of the bell chimed.

"Melinda!" Mary Ann called in her perky voice as she strode over to me, her honey-blond curls bouncing over her shoulders. She glanced at the glass case. "You looked like a caged tiger eyeing her prey. Are they really *that* good?"

I gasped, humiliated that my weakness was so blatantly obvious. "I have no idea what you're talking about," I lied.

"Those." She pointed toward Bernie's oh-so-tempting chocolate marshmallow fudge bars that screamed my name from inside the case. "You're practically drooling."

"No, I'm not," I lied for the second time in under a minute, and a coat of sweat took up residence on my forehead. I needed to maintain control. No, I needed the fudge bar. . . My head started to spin.

"May I help you?" A young woman's irritated voice caught my attention.

I whipped around and gaped. Instead of Bernie's familiar face with his hazel eyes and graying temples, a brunette barista with bright streaks of purple in her hair stood behind the counter, staring at me with an expression of impatience.

I blinked at her. I'd been so focused on myself that I hadn't noticed the owner was missing from his usual routine. "Where's Bernie?"

She frowned. "I have no idea."

"But he mans the register every day," I pointed out. Bernie had never missed a day of work in all the time I'd known him—not even when his wife divorced him for greener pastures (aka: a Parisian guy who'd invited her to run away to France with him *permanently*).

"Sorry to disappoint you. Would you like to order or what?"

"Um . . ." I glanced behind the girl for any sign of Bernie, but didn't spot him. My stomach bubbled with worry. What if something bad had happened to him? I'd grown up coming to Bernie's Bakery daily and he was like a second dad to me.

Trying not to freak out about Bernie, I sucked in a breath, knowing I couldn't regress into my bad fudge bar habit with Mary Ann standing there to witness it. That would be too humiliating. "I'd like a non-fat latte with sugar-free caramel syrup and . . . one bran muffin, please."

Mary Ann tugged on my arm. "Just order the freaking fudge bar."

The woman paused, holding her tongs mid-air, then gave a meaningful glance at the line behind Mary Ann and me. "Did you want to change your order?" she asked.

"I'll stick with the bran muffin, plus whatever she's having." Knowing I really shouldn't revisit the bad habits of my former life, I turned to Mary Ann. "I don't want the fudge bar, but get whatever you want. It's on me."

"You *know* you wanted it. But, whatever." She rolled her eyes then ordered a mocha with extra whip and a chocolate croissant. She handed the barista her credit card. "My treat, actually."

My mouth dropped open, because she'd just bought me a pricey dinner last night and I needed to do something back for her. "No, I can—"

"Too late." Mary Ann waved a hand, then gazed down at my outfit. "You look nice. Do you have an interview this morning? Or are you going to another temp job?"

"Neither," I said, touched that she'd treated me yet again, and given me a compliment on how I looked. I picked a piece of cat hair off my black suit jacket covering the red silk blouse I'd tucked into matching pants. I'd styled my blond mane until no stray hair was out of place and I'd applied my make-up to perfection, but only because these had been daily habits since I'd vowed to lose my ugly duckling reputation. "After seven weeks of low-paying temp jobs, I've reached a dead end. Everyone hiring for a customer service representative has told me I have too much experience."

Mary Ann's nose wrinkled. "Uh, isn't experience a good thing?"

"You'd think." I lifted the brown and white-checkered plate holding my bran muffin, then picked up my coffee cup. "But that's probably the reason Rich Woodward laid me off from his company. I was the lead customer service rep at the top of the pay scale, and he was cutting back on expenses."

"That makes no sense." Her tone rose as if in confusion as she followed me toward a bistro table by the front window. "If you're one of his most valuable employees, then why would he lay you off?"

"To make his business look more profitable on a balance sheet." I slid into the chair across from her. "I'm guessing Rich is getting ready to sell his company. It's the only thing that adds up. He laid off your sister from her office manager job, too, and rolled her duties into the human resources manager position."

"Yeah. Poor Kaitlin's been so stressed out."

"I can imagine." A flicker of jealousy ran through me that she'd said the human resource manager's name so casually as if they were good friends. Much like my school days, I'd never been part of the female in-group at Woodward Systems Corporation. But my roommate,

Ginger, had been besties with everyone. Apparently, so had her sister.

"Hello, hotness!" Mary Ann's sultry tone pulled me from my thoughts.

"Hotness?" I repeated, following Mary Ann's gaze out the window to where a guy on a motorcycle pulled to a stop in front of the bakery. He wore a black leather jacket over his broad shoulders, snug-fitting jeans, and black boots. He dismounted facing the bike, then turned in our direction as he pulled his helmet off.

Hotness was *not* a strong enough word.

Dark layered hair fell across this guy's brow, accentuating the lightness of his jade-green eyes. His narrow jaw complimented full lips that seemed sensual, even from this far away. He was a mixture of style and danger that could tempt any woman to hop on the back of his bike and ride wherever he wanted to go.

"Not my type." I tried to keep my voice even since I suddenly felt short of breath. I'd been interested in a bad boy once before, and he'd left me heartbroken and alone. Not something I cared to repeat. Actually, this guy looked kind of familiar. Maybe he'd been on a local TV station or something.

"That guy is every woman's fantasy." Mary Ann made a humming sound as she stared at him, then she glanced over at me. "Why do you like to deny yourself the fun stuff? Fudge. *Fling.*"

"I'm not a person who lives on the edge," I said, knowing a girl like Mary Ann, who gives in to her every whim, wouldn't understand my preference for stable men or the treacherous history between me and those fudge bars. "I have more important things on my mind, anyway."

"Like what?" she asked, breaking off a piece of croissant and popping it into her mouth. She stared at me with a gaze so sincere, it felt like she actually cared.

I'd never had a friend I felt comfortable confiding in, but she genuinely seemed concerned. I suddenly found myself wanting to tell her everything I was going through. I took a deep breath. "Well, I—"

"Jiminy Cricket!" a male voice shouted, then a splattering of papers fluttered across our table as a man's body hit the floor beside me, face first.

"Are you all right, sir?" I knelt next to the peppered-haired man as his nose rose off the floor revealing thick black glasses perched crookedly. My eyes widened. "Bernie? Is that you?"

"I'm not sure who's asking." He pressed his palms against the floor, pushed himself up onto his elbows, then tilted his head my way. "Melinda Morgan. I'd ask where you've been hiding, but I look rather ridiculous right now."

"Let me help you up." I held his arm firmly while he stood. Mary Ann fished up the papers he'd accidentally thrown and handed them to me. I glanced down at what appeared to be a stack of résumés then gave them to Bernie. "Are you all right?"

He brushed off his pants. "It's good to see you. How's your mother?"

"Fine," I said, automatically. But, in truth, the last time I'd seen her she'd looked pretty depressed. That's when I'd told her to stop painting those ridiculous ceramic hot air balloons and that she needed to get over my dad's death once and for all. I also told her it might be time for therapy. She'd said she would think about it, but neither of us had brought it up again. "I'm going to visit my mom after this, actually."

Bernie adjusted his thick black glasses. "I'm glad to hear she's doing well. Please say hello to her for me. Now I'll let you finish your breakfast in peace," he said, giving a polite nod to Mary Ann. "I apologize for the interruption."

Mary Ann smiled. "No worries here."

I watched Bernie walk away with what seemed like a limp. Poor guy. That had been a hard fall and he seemed pretty shaken up. I held my finger up to Mary Ann, then strode over to the table where Bernie had sat down. "Why aren't you behind the register today? Who's the woman behind the counter with the pretty purple streaks in her hair? What are all of those résumés for?"

"These are tough questions to answer." He removed his glasses and rubbed his eyes. "But I've known you too long to hide it from you. . . I've been sick. The doctors say I need to stop working—permanently."

I brought my hand to my chest. "I'm so sorry to hear about your health. They think you'll get better if you retire?"

"That is their opinion." He set the résumés down on

the table, his expression tired and worn. "They say I need stop working immediately and rest, but I don't have anyone to run the bakery. I hired Avery last week for extra register help—she's working behind the counter right now and seems to be doing a good job. Don't you think?"

"She's . . . capable." I didn't want to add to Bernie's worries so I refrained from telling him how the long line seemed to stress her out and that her impatience showed big-time. Since I'd been in customer service for years, I knew that the way the patron is treated is practically as important as the product itself but this girl Avery obviously didn't understand that concept. "What are all of the résumés for then?"

"Responses to the manager position I advertised in the paper." His expression drooped further, making him appear defeated. "I need someone to manage the bakery, including the accounting, purchasing, day-to-day operations and, of course, the baking."

"That shouldn't be too hard to find," I said, glancing at the large stack of applicants he had to choose from. He'd taught me all of those roles when I was a college student working for him so surely he'd find someone quickly. "Did any qualified candidates apply?"

"Many have the proper experience, yes. But this bakery has been the love of my life for almost twenty years. I can't hand her over to just anybody. There will need to be many interviews, perhaps background checks. I need a manager who I trust completely. Otherwise, instead of improving my health, I could have a heart attack."

Every cell in my body froze. "The doctors said that's a possibility?"

Hanging his head, he nodded. "I've been having heart palpitations."

I gasped. "Oh, Bernie."

"You can see now why I'm tripping over my own two feet." He gestured toward the floor. "I don't know what to do. The doctor tells me that I need to rest completely for at least two weeks, but how can I relax at all if I'm leaving my beloved bakery in the hands of a virtual stranger?"

My heart squeezed. "If it's the doctor's advice, then you must find a way to rest for the next two weeks. You can't mess around with health. That's all there is to it."

He shook his head, then sifted through the papers. "In order to relax, I need someone I trust. But how will I find a person like this on such short notice?"

I bit my lip. Volunteering to run Bernie's Bakery was the absolute *last* thing I should do. It wouldn't pay nearly as much as a job in the business world, which I needed to regain my independence, and it would be a plus if I could afford a place to live where cat hair didn't coat the carpet. I didn't envy Ginger having pets, because the pain I'd felt when I'd lost my childhood dog, Checkers, was nothing I cared to feel again. I even kept my distance from her little meowzers so I wouldn't get attached to them.

I glanced down at Bernie, who was staring hopelessly at the résumé on top of the pile. Dark circles stood out beneath his eyes, his skin looked pale, and his handsome face seemed to have aged a decade since the last time I'd seen him.

"I'll do it," I blurted, knowing Bernie's health was at stake. He had always been there for me. Shortly after his wife had left him and moved away with their son (aka: my former best friend), my dad had died. Bernie had come to the funeral, offering to help with whatever my mom and I needed. He'd also sent us a basket of baked goodies every week for a year. He'd been an amazing friend over the years and a wonderful father figure.

I would not desert him in his time of need.

His eyes widened as he slowly lifted his gaze to meet mine. "You'll do what?"

"I will manage your bakery for two weeks, while you rest and get healthy," I said, ignoring the look of confusion Mary Ann was throwing at me.

"Thank you, Melinda." He smiled, his eyes watering for a moment. "You're very kind to offer to help, but you have a blossoming career. Your mom has told me about each and every one of your promotions. She couldn't be more proud of you. I can't let you sacrifice your success for me."

"Apparently my mom hasn't told you about my current status," I said, thinking about how odd that was, since she usually stopped in several times each week to grab a cup of coffee and chat with Bernie. "When's the last time you spoke with her?"

"I'm afraid it has been awhile since she's come in.

Just like with you. Truthfully, I've been a little worried about you both."

My brows came together. I hadn't been coming to this neighborhood because I was trying desperately to find a new job. But why had *she* stopped coming into Bernie's? Especially since my mom was the queen of routine.

I took a deep breath. "My employer laid me off seven weeks ago. I've been searching for a permanent job, which I still haven't found. So it's not a problem for me to work here temporarily while you get the rest you need. I can start today after I drop by my mom's house," I said, my nerves frazzled at the thought of asking to dip into my inheritance money.

His brows rose quizzically. "Are you absolutely sure it wouldn't inconvenience you too much?"

My eyes blurred, touched that he was thinking of me when his own situation was so desperate. "It's only two weeks, and I'm happy to do it. Really. You remember how much I loved working here."

"If you're absolutely sure." His expression filled with emotion as he rose to his feet, grabbed my hand, and placed it between his two palms. "This is the answer to my prayers. I'll pay you the same rate as I would a permanent manager."

"It's a deal." I squeezed his hand, smiling at the relief evident his eyes. "This afternoon I'll come back and you can catch me up on all of your current procedures. And don't worry while you're gone, because your bakery will be in good hands."

"With you running the show, I have no doubt." He released my hand, picked up his stack of papers, and turned back to me. "If Nate gives you any trouble because I put you in charge of managing the bakery instead of him, please let me know and I'll take care of it. He's being moody, as usual."

"Um, Nate?" A chill ran down my spine. Bernie couldn't be talking about his rebellious son who'd moved to Paris with his mom when I was fourteen, leaving me with the bittersweet memory of my first real kiss and a shattered heart.

"Nate returned to Sacramento a couple weeks ago due to my condition. He'd been surfing in Bali when I called to inform him of the doctor's findings. You know he's a photographer of extreme adventures, right? His business is even online now."

My mouth had opened, but no words were coming out. Nate was here? In Sac?

"Anyway, he insists on running the bakery for me, but he has no experience. Plus, unlike you, he's never shown any interest in the bakery. So I know he's only offering in order to be helpful. He much prefers one grand adventure after another, as you'll recall. I'm sure you will be a good influence on him, since you value stability."

Me? Influence bullheaded Nate Carter? Not likely. Against my better judgment, I'd given in to my secret feelings for him the summer before freshman year in high school when he'd cornered me on the swing set at the park by my house. I'd gone to the park to be alone since we'd just put down my sweet dog, Checkers—named after my favorite childhood game.

The memory of our kiss flooded my brain, sending tingles down my arms. Then my stomach steeled. One amazing kiss, then I'd never heard from him again. Not even so much as a postcard since he'd moved away a week later.

My stomach churned at the thought of seeing Nate, but I couldn't let it show. Any additional stress would only worsen Bernie's condition.

Unwillingly, my fists balled and my eyes narrowed. "Oh, I can handle Nate."

"That sounds like an enticing proposition," a distinctive male voice came from behind me. "But shouldn't I at least take you out to lunch first?"

I spun around to find myself face-to-face with the leather jacket-wearing hottie that Mary Ann had called every woman's fantasy. Our gazes locked and I stared into jade-green eyes that flickered with emotion. My breath caught in my throat.

Standing before me was Bernie's son, Nate Carter. My first crush and greatest heartbreak all rolled into one. And I'd just agreed to manage his dad's bakery for the next two weeks, which meant I'd be stuck seeing plenty of him.

I totally should've ordered the fudge bar.

Chapter Two

As I stared into Nate Carter's twinkling jade-green eyes, something stirred in my belly, and it took every ounce of effort I had to maintain a composed demeanor. If a guy breaks your heart, you don't want him to fall off his motorcycle or anything, but you certainly don't want your legs to turn to jelly just because he's standing in front of you thirteen years later.

So *not* right.

"Hello, Nate." My tone was even with just the right hint of friendly so he wouldn't guess how he'd ripped my heart to smithereens when we were young, or how he still affected me now for that matter. I took a deep breath. "Welcome back to town."

"Thanks." The corner of his mouth lifted, making him look even sexier, which shouldn't have been possible since the guy was already the definition of smoking hot. "It's good to be back."

A buzzing sound came from Bernie's direction and he pulled his cell phone from his pocket, then scanned the screen. "If you'll both excuse me, I have to take this. I'll see you this afternoon, Melinda. Thank you again."

"No problem." I smiled at Bernie then shifted my gaze back to Nate, who was staring right at me. My tummy did a little flip. Gulp. "I trust you're having a nice visit?"

"Getting better all the time." His gaze left my face and traveled down my body then slowly made his way back up again, leaving a trail of heat in its wake. "I can't believe it's been this long since we've seen each other. You look beautiful, as always."

"Thank you." My cheeks flushed at his compliment and I hoped he didn't notice. I'd lost all of my extra "fudge" pounds since he'd last seen me at fourteen. It gave me goosebumps that he'd thought I was beautiful back when I was curvier, too.

"I have to head to work now." Mary Ann's peppy voice seemed to come out of nowhere. She suddenly appeared at my side, extending her hand toward Nate. "I'm Melinda's friend, Mary Ann."

"Nate." He smiled warmly and grasped her hand in his. "Any friend of Melinda's is a friend of mine."

She placed her other hand over her chest. "Gorgeous *and* sweet? I hope we're going to be seeing more of you."

"I'm sure Nate has better, more adventurous things to do than hang with us," I said, as a flitter of jealousy rolled through me, which was ridiculous. It meant nothing to me if Nate shook the hand of my adorable single friend, who had earlier referred to him as every woman's fantasy. At least I tried to convince myself it didn't bother me.

"I'll definitely be around," he said, releasing her hand and facing me. "We have a lot of catching up to do, don't we?"

I turned to Mary Ann. "I'll see you later. Thanks again for the coffee."

"Anytime." She backed up a few feet until she was standing behind Nate, looked him up and down, and gave me the thumbs up sign. Then she held her hand to the side of her head with her thumb toward her ear and her pinky toward her mouth, in the universal sign for "call me."

"It was nice to see you, Nate. But I really should be going, too." I forced a smile, then turned to my table and gathered my untouched bran muffin in a paper napkin. I started toward the door.

He stepped in front of me, blocking my path. "We need to have lunch."

I sucked in a deep breath, unwittingly inhaling the scent of his leather jacket since he was only standing a few inches away. The distinctive aroma conjured an insane image of me swinging my leg over the back of Nate's motorcycle and wrapping my arms around his waist as we zoomed down the street with my hair flying behind me. Weird.

I'd never ridden a motorcycle and didn't plan to ride one ever. I especially wouldn't ride one with Nate, though. "Thanks, but I can't have lunch with you."

He peered down at me. "Dinner then."

"Sorry." I shook my head, adjusting the purse strap on my shoulder. "It's nice that you're visiting your dad, but I'm sure you'll be off to Paris soon. Or Bali. Or wherever the wind blows you. Then I'll never hear from you again."

An unreadable look crossed his face. "I'm here indefinitely. We have a lot to talk about. Can't you make time to catch up with an old friend?"

My heart squeezed. A friend would've written or called, not disappeared from my life without a word—especially after the kiss we'd shared.

"Look, I've agreed to manage the bakery for a little while so your dad can get the rest he needs. I'm sure we'll see each other around." Or not.

He tilted his head, giving me an inquisitive side-glance. "What if the bakery sells before we get the chance?"

"Well, then . . ." I started to step around him, then my mind processed what he'd just said and I stopped in my tracks. I spun around so fast, the muffin slipped out of my hand and bounced across the floor. "Bernie's thinking of selling the bakery?"

"He already put it on the market." He squatted down and retrieved my breakfast casualty from under a bistro table where it had bumped into some man's unsuspecting loafer. "His Realtor, Wendy Watts, is putting the "for sale" sign up tomorrow. She's on billboards all over town and is supposed to be the best in Sacramento."

My heart dropped to the floor, and my brain swirled trying to make sense of what he was telling me. I shook my head, because the possibility of Bernie selling his bakery did not compute. "But your dad's going through a stack of résumés to hire a manager. Why would he do that if he's selling?"

"In addition to selling the building, he's hoping someone will buy the business and keep it going. That's his dream, anyway." Nate tossed the dirty muffin into a nearby trash can, then returned with a crease between his brows. "I thought he'd explained all of this to you."

"No." Tears burned behind my eyes, and I blinked rapidly to keep them at bay as I fought for composure. I couldn't imagine Bernie not being here every day. My throat started to close, so I made a show of checking my watch. I had to get of here before I broke down. "I'm late to meet my mom. I have to go. Bye, Nate."

"Melinda . . ."

I heard his voice behind me, but I hurried to the exit before I lost it. The purple-haired barista shouted my name as I dashed by, and shoved a basket of baked goods over the counter, saying Bernie had put it together for my mom. Of course he had. That's what he *often* did.

But that wouldn't happen anymore—not once

Bernie's Bakery was sold to the highest bidder. My throat tightened even further. With the basket in one hand, I pulled open the yellow door with the other, and the familiar *ding-a-ling* of the bell chimed overhead. A wave of nausea rolled through me and I rushed to my car.

I unlocked the door and climbed behind the wheel, but my hand was too shaky to get the key in the ignition. My eyes watered and my chest pounded, so I leaned back in the seat trying to take deep calming breaths. Immediately my gaze darted to the building on the corner. Big white letters with a thick brown outline decorated the center of the window, spelling out "Bernie's Bakery" in a cheerful font.

That bakery was a neighborhood icon. It had been a place of joy when I was growing up back when Nate and I were best friends, a place of comfort after my dad had died, and it still felt like my home away from home. But soon the bakery would be sold and its fate would be up to the new owner, who could turn it into a yoga studio or a clothing boutique or whatever they wanted.

The mere thought of Bernie's Bakery shutting down had absolutely devastated to me. I couldn't imagine how heartbroken I'd be when it actually happened.

****

Completely crushed by the news that Bernie was selling his bakery, I had to force myself to concentrate on the road ahead as I pulled my convertible away from the curb by Bernie's Bakery. I cruised through "The Fabulous Forties" neighborhood in East Sacramento, heading to my mom's house to ask for a small chunk of the inheritance funds I had never wanted to touch just so I could pay next month's rent.

Even in my sad state, I had to admit that it made sense that Bernie would sell his bakery. His health was at stake, which was why even his audacious son had (annoyingly) returned after all those years of being away. I also supposed Bernie was close to an early retirement age. But I couldn't imagine a life where Bernie's Bakery didn't exist. There *must* be a way to ensure its survival.

As I continued through the neighborhood I'd grown up in, my gaze darted around and I admired the grand custom homes built in the early twentieth century. Tudor-style homes. Dutch farmhouses. Mediterranean villas. A homey feeling encompassed me, along with the familiar longing to own one of these beautiful houses myself someday.

Not likely, at the rate I was going. Sigh.

I pulled into the driveway of the two-story brick colonial revival-style home I'd grown up in, and parked beside the sweeping green lawn. Then my gaze fell to the basket of baked goods sitting on my front passenger seat that Bernie had so lovingly put together for my mom.

Bernie's bakery hadn't just been a job for him. He'd loved spending his time there every day, and his choice of business had made him happy. Unlike me, who was searching for another customer service job I didn't really enjoy. I found myself wishing I'd chosen a career that I loved as much Bernie had loved his.

Wait a minute. . . .

A nervous burst of laughter escaped as an idea started percolating in my brain. My mind flew back to all of the good times I'd had when I'd worked at Bernie's Bakery during college. I remembered the peace that would come over me, while baking during the early morning hours before the rest of the world was awake. I'd loved greeting and chatting with the regular customers, who had inevitably felt like an extended part of my family. I still ran into some of them from time to time.

Working at the bakery had been *so* much fun.

What if I bought the bakery?

Suddenly, the solution made perfect sense. I knew what I had to do. Gripping the handle of Bernie's basket of goodies with my hand, I jumped out of the car and hurried up the walkway toward my mom's front door. I didn't need to just dip into the inheritance funds my dad had left me so I could get through the next month. I needed to accept the whole shebang so I could buy Bernie's Bakery!

Adrenaline blasted through me, and I knew with every ounce of my being that this was the correct decision. I'd never felt right accepting money that had resulted from my dad's death, but now I realized what an incredible gift he'd left for me. This generous gift would completely change the direction of my life. I'd finally be spending my days doing something meaningful that I loved—just like Bernie had done.

And even though it was such a large sum, I knew my mom wouldn't have a problem handing over all of the funds to me. She'd offered it up many times over the years, practically trying to force me to take it. Wearing an excited smile that I hadn't felt in weeks, months, or maybe even years, I pressed the doorbell.

I couldn't wait to tell my mom about my plan to buy Bernie's Bakery. She'd be happy, I figured, since Bernie's had featured predominantly in her life, too. During my childhood, my mom had always been impeccably dressed, attending elegant social functions every weekend. Whenever she was in charge of an event, she always had it catered with Bernie's delicious delicacies. She'd enjoyed hosting parties herself as well, and ordered all of the food from the bakery because his delectable goodies were the best around.

Not like she'd had anything catered by Bernie lately, though. Once my dad had passed away in that ridiculously tragic hot air balloon accident, my mom had stopped leaving the house and instead spent her days painting ceramic hot air balloons as if she were trying to bring him back to life or something.

In addition to abandoning her social life, her designer put-together look had slowly declined to the point that, seven weeks ago, I'd arrived to find her wearing a wrinkled sweat suit covered with splotches of paint. She'd had long, gray roots too as if she had been skipping her monthly beauty salon treatments, even though she used to be religious about those appointments.

That was why I'd suggested she go see a therapist. She'd blown me off with an annoyed look, so I hadn't brought it up again in all of our conversations. I knew it was her life to live how she wanted, but deep down I didn't feel like she was happy anymore.

Hearing footsteps approaching the door, I bounced on my heels, anxious to tell her about my plan to buy Bernie's Bakery. Maybe that would help show her that change could be good. Then she could *change* out of those dreadful sweats, which I deeply believed belonged in the garbage can.

The front door opened, and my eyes widened in shock. "Mom . . .?"

"Hello, Melinda." She smiled, and I resisted the urge to pinch myself. Instead of sweats, she wore a peacock-blue button-up blouse, white pants, and the pearl necklace that had belonged to my grandmother. Her hair was the lovely ash blonde her hair-stylist favored, only she wore it down instead of pulled back. "I'm glad you were available to come over this morning. I have a lot I need to discuss with you."

"You look so different," I blurted out, then realized that was the understatement of the year. This was not the same woman whose sweat suit had seemed permanently plastered to her body, nor was this the same woman from my childhood who had preferred neutral colors and wearing her hair in a bun at the nape of her neck. My mom had completely transformed.

"Well, I should hope I look different. I've been going to therapy twice a week for almost two months."

My eyes welled with tears. "You've been seeing a therapist?"

"What else could I do when my daughter seemed worried about me?" She pulled me into a hug so strong and comforting that I wanted to bury my head into her shoulder like I'd done when I was little. "I've had a hard time letting your dad go, sweetheart."

When she released me, I shifted my stance on the foyer's marble floor. "And now?"

She smiled wistfully. "I'll always love him, but I have to start living my life again. In that regard, I have a few important matters to talk about with you. Let's sit in the family room. I've made us some coffee."

"Before I forget . . ." I handed her the basket of baked goods. "Bernie asked me to bring these to you. I just came from the bakery."

"How thoughtful." Her eyes lit up as she lifted the brown and white–checkered cloth and peeked inside. Knowing Bernie, they were all of my mom's favorites. Zucchini bread. Almond croissants. Carrot cake. She laced her arm through mine, then led me toward the family room. "How is Bernie?"

We passed by the grandfather clock next to the staircase, which began to chime the ninth hour, then we stepped into the family room. Numerous ceramic hot air balloons cheerfully occupied shelves around the room, each balloon and basket hand-painted in a unique color pattern by my mom. On a table in the corner of the room sat a ceramic urn with tiny hot air balloons painted around its middle. Inside the urn were my dad's ashes.

Having his remains here had creeped me out at first,

but I'd grown used to saying hi to Dad when I came in the room. I touched the hot air balloon urn lightly with the tips of my fingers, my throat tightening a bit before I remembered my mom had asked about Bernie.

I faced her, and swallowed. "Bernie's not well, actually."

Her brows knitted together as she stopped beside the buffet table. "What do you mean he's not well?"

"It's pretty serious." I didn't want to sugar coat it, but I felt bad that her expression had changed from relaxed to worried. "His doctor advised him to stop working and rest for two weeks due to heart palpitations. It's so serious that even Nate is back in town." *Looking hotter than ever*, I thought, but obviously didn't say aloud.

She set the basket of baked goods on the buffet table, next to her rose-patterned china coffee pot and matching coffee cups and saucers. "I need to call Bernie," she said.

"I'm sure he'd like that." I pushed the image of Nate out of my mind and sat down on the sofa. I twisted my hands together, nervous about what I was bringing up next. "There's something else I want to tell you. It's kind of a huge decision I've made, actually."

My mom continued to stare at the wicker basket on the mahogany buffet table as if she hadn't heard me.

"Mom?"

She lifted her head slowly. "Hmm?"

I frowned, wondering if she was more distraught over Bernie's condition than I'd anticipated. "If you're worried about Bernie, you don't need to be. I'm managing his bakery for the next two weeks so he'll be able to rest."

"Well, that's a relief." She smoothed out the checkered towel lying across the top of the basket until it was without a wrinkle. "He loves his bakery, though. It will be hard for him to be away. You'll need to call him every day to assure him everything's going smoothly. And make sure that nice boy Nate sends a basket of freshly baked bread daily, too. That will cheer Bernie up."

I mentally huffed. A "nice" boy would've called me after the kiss we'd shared. The thought of asking Nate Carter for *anything* irritated me. If it would be good for Bernie to have freshly baked bread delivered, then I'd rather take it to him myself.

"Fine," I said, annoyed that she'd gotten so bossy all of a sudden. "But there's something else I need to talk to you about. Bernie has decided to sell the bakery. I know I've turned down the inheritance money from Dad repeatedly, but I've decided to finally accept the money so I can buy the bakery. I'll keep it open and thriving. Isn't that fantastic?"

"Uh . . ." Instead of excitement or even answering me, her face paled, and she stood abruptly. She went over to the buffet table and poured two cups of coffee, then set them on coasters on the coffee table. "I don't have that sugar-free syrup you love so much, but would you like cream or sugar?"

"Black's fine." I waved a hand. "But didn't you hear what I said? I've found my calling. Customer service was always just a paycheck for me. Owning Bernie's Bakery is now my dream. I haven't found out the exact price yet, but I remember how much the inheritance money was over a decade ago. I'm sure that would be more than enough. Since you'd invested it, it's probably even gone up since then. Right?"

"Quite a bit, actually." She sat back down again, but

instead of reaching for her coffee cup she rubbed her palms against her thighs. "Before we talk about the bakery, I have some things to tell you."

I didn't like how her expression had grown distant and how she seemed to look everywhere but at me. "What is it, Mom?"

She cleared her throat. "First, I'm going to have your father's ashes scattered over the Sierras from a hot air balloon. I'm trying to find a company that will do it, which is proving more difficult than you could imagine."

I choked on my coffee. "You're spreading Daddy's ashes?" My gaze automatically flew to the ceramic urn, to make sure it was still there. "Why would you suddenly decide to do that after thirteen years? Don't I get a say in this?"

"Your dad left me a letter saying that's what he wants." She pressed her lips together, causing the lines on either side of her mouth to deepen. Then she reached into her handbag and pulled out a white envelope, still sealed. "When our lawyer gave me your dad's will after he passed away, she also handed me an envelope, and told me it was a personal letter from him."

A stampede of needles pricked across my chest, and down my arms. "You never told me he wrote you a letter."

"That's because I didn't have the heart to open it." She dropped her gaze, staring at the envelope she held in her manicured hands, then she glanced up at me. "It's been sitting in my nightstand drawer all of these years. Part of me felt like if I read his final letter to me, there really would be no turning back. I'm sure that sounds silly."

"It doesn't." My throat tightened as I thought back to how my dad had died so unexpectedly. He had left early in the morning for his big hot air balloon adventure, and hadn't returned. We never got to say good-bye. "But how do you know that he wanted his ashes scattered in the Sierras?" I pointed to the envelope in her hand. "The letter's still sealed."

"After talking with my therapist, I decided it was time for me to read his letter. I read it last night before I called you." She fingered the envelope, then swiveled it around so the front faced me. "This envelope was *inside* the envelope for me. It's addressed to you."

Chills vibrated through me. I stared at the handwritten script on the front of the envelope: *For Melinda*

What the . . .?

"That's for me?" My eyes burned as I reached for the envelope, staring at the two words on the front, which were written in my dad's familiar handwriting. Covering my mouth with my hand, I turned the envelope over and confirmed it was still sealed.

She laid her hand over mine and squeezed. "If I'd known there was a letter inside for you then I would've opened mine right away. I'm sorry, sweetheart."

I closed my eyes and nodded, knowing my mom would never have kept something like this from me if she'd known. A letter from my dad after all of these years. "I can't believe he wrote me a letter," I whispered.

"There's something else." Her tone was ominous.

My eyes popped open. "What?"

She gnawed on her bottom lip for a long pause. "In his letter to me, your dad said not to give you the inheritance money until you finish his *Carpe Diem* list."

"His *what?*" I gaped at the envelope as if it had suddenly grown fangs.

"A list of 'seize the day' tasks that he wants you to complete in order to have a more fruitful life." She took a quick sip of her coffee as if she needed to be recharged. "I don't know what tasks he made for you, but he left a *Carpe Diem* list for me, as well."

My brows came together and I held up my palm. "Let me get this straight. When I turned eighteen, you told me I could have my inheritance money. Now, almost a decade later, you're saying I can't have the funds until I've completed Dad's *Carpe Diem* list even though we don't know what's on it?"

She raised her shoulders, and her mouth puckered. "Don't be upset with me. It wasn't *my* choice."

I waved the envelope in the air. "What if he wants me to see the Great Wall of China first? Or hike Mount Everest? We are talking about Dad here. I could lose the chance to buy Bernie's Bakery!"

Her penciled brows drew together. "I'm so sorry, sweetheart. But it's his final wish. You know I can't go against that, and I should hope you wouldn't want me to."

"Well, that's just great." I stood, leaving my coffee virtually untouched. "I finally have a professional dream, and now it's going to slip through my fingers because I can't complete a list of tasks that I hadn't known about until five minutes ago."

She rose to her feet, and stepped toward me. "Sweetheart, calm down. Open the envelope and see what's on the list. Maybe they're tasks you can do quickly."

"Oh, please." I shoved the envelope in my purse, then crossed my arms over my chest. "Dad was the king of adventure. I'm sure his list includes something like an African safari. I'll be eaten by a lion before I ever get the chance to buy the bakery—if it's not sold and turned into a day spa by then."

My eyes burned. This was suddenly all too much. Bernie's health problems. Nate's return. Spreading my dad's ashes. The inheritance money I hadn't wanted and now wasn't allowed to have. The letter from my dad to my mom. His letter to *me*. . . .

I threw my hands in the air. "I have to go."

"Melinda, wait—"

"I'll talk to you later, Mom." I turned and hurried down the hallway because I couldn't take any more right now. I walked out the front door, then got into my car and started the engine. My mom had closed herself off from me after my dad had died and her prime concern had been painting a gazillion ceramic hot air balloons. That's why this letter from my dad hadn't appeared until now, which had to be the worst timing ever.

I backed out of the driveway unable to believe my dream was being crushed only an hour after I'd discovered what it was. How tragic was that? I pressed my foot on the gas and zoomed down the tree-lined street.

There was only one place I wanted to be right now.

With tears spilling down my face, I rounded the corner, and brought my convertible to a stop against the curb at my childhood park. I swiped at my cheeks, then retrieved the envelope from my purse and left the bag on the floor of the car.

Gripping the envelope in my hand, I marched toward the swing set, which had always been my favorite spot to sit and think when I was sad.

Fresh tears escaped, blurring my sight as I approached the edge of the sandbox that enclosed the swing set area. I stepped over the wooden box and my heels sank into the sand as I plodded toward my swing. Then I glanced up, gasped, and came to an abrupt halt.

In front of me was Nate Carter, sitting on my favorite swing.

Chapter Three

Only one swing set occupied the large sandbox at the park, and it contained two black seats, each hanging from a linked chain attached to an overhead wooden beam. Nate was sitting in the swing to my right, which happened to be my favorite.

He'd ditched the leather jacket and was wearing a short-sleeved shirt—one that showed off his muscular arms—and snug-fit jeans. With the heels of my shoes sinking further into the sandbox, I gaped at him in shock, and watched his gaze lift to meet mine.

Our gazes locked and an electric current ran through my belly, giving me a strong sense of déjà vu. I had to remind myself that I wasn't fourteen, my dog hadn't just died, and Nate wasn't about to kiss me. Far from it. In truth, it was probably a toss-up as to which one of us looked more surprised to see the other.

"What are you doing here?" I quickly swiped under my eyes, hoping I didn't have black lines of mascara streaked across my face.

He jumped to his feet. "That's the same question I was about to ask you."

"I came here to be alone," I said, hoping he'd take the hint and find someplace else to do, well, whatever it was he was doing. It was hard enough that I'd have to see him at the bakery for the next two weeks. I certainly didn't need him here right now when I came to my sacred spot for emotional comfort, not distress.

"Well, I was here first." He backed himself up against the seat of the swing, lifted his legs, then swung forward with a playful grin. "But you can stay if you'd like. Hop onto the other swing. I don't mind your company."

With a heavy sigh, I kicked my heels off, then climbed onto the left swing. "Since I can't have the park to myself, I'd appreciate it if you would pretend I'm not here. I'd like to be alone with my thoughts."

"Not a problem." He grinned, then faced forward and pumped his legs to go higher.

Trying to erase the image of his alluring grin, I backed up on my tippy-toes, and sat in the seat. Then I lifted my legs and glided forward. The cool wind whipped across my cheeks and I closed my eyes, waiting for the comfort to wash over me. It didn't happen.

Most likely because Nate was here. Sigh.

"What's that in your hand?" His tone sounded curious.

"Nothing." I twisted toward him, and tightened my grip on the sealed envelope, knowing I couldn't read it now, not with him peering over at me. "Besides, you agreed not to talk to me. Remember?"

He had the decency to appear contrite. "Yeah, but you look upset. And this is where you come when something's bothering you. So why don't you tell me about it?"

"No, thanks."

"Come on." He gave me a side-glance, flashing his gorgeous jade-green eyes at me in an endearing way. "Don't you remember all of the things we used to share?"

I started to smile, remembering the secrets we would tell each other growing up. Then I recalled how he'd kissed me, then promptly disappeared from my life without so much as a sticky note. The corners of my mouth turned downward. "That's when we were kids. We're grown up now."

"Yeah, it has been a long time since we've seen each other." He glanced away for a moment, then turned back to me wearing a somber expression. "After the last time I saw you, I came home from the park and my parents told me they were splitting."

"I had no idea that's when you found out," I said, wondering if he hadn't called me after that day because he'd been too devastated over his parents' divorce. Still, he could've sent a letter once things had calmed down.

He nodded. "They also told me that my mom was moving to France with some guy I hadn't known about, and I had to decide if I was going with her or staying here with my dad."

"How awful." I'd heard through the grapevine that his mom's relationship with that French dude hadn't lasted. But she'd stayed in Paris and eventually remarried.

His brows furrowed, then he shrugged. "My dad's always been the strong one, so I decided my mom needed me more. That was the hardest year of my life."

"Mine, too." I understood all too well what it felt like to have your family torn apart.

"I was sorry to hear about your dad." His voice was wrought with sincerity. Then he leaned toward me and placed his hand on my arm. "He was an amazing person."

"Thanks." Even through my sleeve, my skin felt warm where his fingers wrapped around my forearm. I felt my emotional walls giving way a bit. The envelope in my hand suddenly felt like lead, and I held it toward him with the top facing upward. "I just came from my mom's house. She found this letter my dad wrote to me before he died."

"She just gave this to you today?" He watched me nod, then lines formed between his brows as his gaze dropped to the envelope. He took it from me and flipped it over as if checking the seal before meeting my gaze again. "You haven't read it?"

"No." I shook my head, surprised that I'd shared something so personal with him. But once we'd started talking it had felt natural to tell him.

"You said you wanted to be alone . . ." He glanced from me to the envelope, and a look of understanding crossed his face. "That's why you came here. To read his letter."

I nodded.

He threw his gaze upward, shaking his head. "And here I've been babbling on like an idiot, thinking you were just trying to get rid of me because . . ." His voice trailed off, then he stood. "I'm sorry, Melinda. I should've given you your space right away."

"Don't worry about it." My heart rate sped up since I could tell he was going to leave and part of me wanted to ask him to stay. We'd been such good friends when we were young, but I'd let my stupid feelings get in the way by kissing him. Otherwise, I wouldn't have been so hurt by him not calling me and would've reached out to him myself when I'd heard his parents were divorcing.

"I'll be at the bakery if you need anything," he said, backing away.

"Thanks." It was on the tip of my tongue to ask him to wait, but he turned and strode across the lawn to the motorcycle I hadn't noticed parked at the curb. Seconds later, it roared to life and he sped down the street.

As soon as he disappeared out of sight, I inhaled a deep breath, then ripped open the envelope. I pulled out a watermarked piece of stationery, customized with an

"E.M." monogram at the top for my dad's name, Edward Morgan. My eyes watered at my dad's familiar handwriting, and I read:

My beautiful princess,

Since you're reading this letter, I've passed on to my next adventure. I'm proud to say I married the love of my life, had you for my daughter, and lived as fully as any man could want or deserve. I am truly thankful for this.

Nothing would make me happier than for you embrace life completely like I did. If you'll indulge Daddy a wish, I have created a Carpe Diem list for you to complete at your earliest opportunity:

1) Rescue a dog.

2) Host a girls' night.

3) Only date someone who leaves you breathless.

4) Fix your biggest regret.

Don't be upset with Daddy for giving you homework. It's only because I believe this list will help you seize more of what life has to offer like you deserve. I left a list for your mother as well. Please take care of each other. My love will be with you both forever.

Always remember that each breath of air is precious, every bird's song is magic, and when you look up to find where the sky is shining brightest blue, know that's where I'll be . . . smiling down at you.

Love,

Daddy

I reread the letter over and over, hot tears spilling over my cheeks. Since he'd died unexpectedly, we never got to say good-bye to each other. Now, in some way, he'd been able to tell me good-bye. But why had he told my mom that my inheritance hinged on my completing this *Carpe Diem* list? He said in this letter that he wanted me to seize life, but instead he'd put up a big blockade to my dream.

I scanned the list again. *Rescue a dog?* Why would he ask me to do such a thing when losing Checkers had been so utterly painful? *Host a girls' night?* Like anyone would show up if I did. He used to bug me to have girl friends over, and I'd rolled my eyes every time. He never did get that I was the queen of being excluded from exactly this kind of event, and he was still pestering me about it from the great beyond.

Only date someone who leaves you breathless? The problem with this task was that the kind of guy to leave me breathless was the exact type of guy to break my heart. Um, hello? Two words: Nate Carter. And *Fix your biggest regret?* That would prove to be a little difficult, considering it would involve going up in a hot air balloon with my dad who happened to be dead.

Wiping my cheeks with the back of my sleeve, my brows furrowed as I wondered how long it would take me to complete this list. Because one thing was for certain: I had to complete this list in time to save the bakery.

****

Bernie and I spent the afternoon together, with him catching me up on all of the bakery's current procedures, which comically hadn't changed that much since I was in college. After confirming that I was fully capable of caring for his business, he finally went home to rest.

I didn't tell Bernie that I wanted to buy the bakery because I wanted to make sure I could complete my dad's *Carpe Diem* list and get my inheritance money first. While Bernie was briefing me, I'd spotted Nate once or twice in the kitchen, but then he disappeared. Part of me wanted to tell him about my dad's letter and my desire to buy the bakery. But I knew the urge to confide in him was just an old habit that had been conjured up by seeing him again.

Avery, Bernie's new barista, had taken the news that I'd be supervising her in stride. Her only concern was whether or not her hours would be cut, and Bernie assured her they wouldn't. When it was time to close up shop, I was getting ready to leave when Avery asked if I'd help her wipe down the tables and clean up. I found her request odd since she didn't strike me as the kind of person who asked for favors.

"I have to admit, I didn't peg you as the type to work in a café." Avery scrubbed a wet cloth over the top of a bistro table, causing the pretty purple knot of hair at the base of her neck to bob back and forth. "More like editor of a fashion magazine or something."

Her tone held humor so I wasn't sure if she meant her comment as a compliment or an insult, but I immediately felt defensive. "Actually, I was the lead customer service rep for one of the top office software companies in

Sacramento."

"Didn't see that one coming," she said, her tone containing that same hint of humor. "What brings you to the world of baked goods?"

"I'm helping Bernie out," I said, since it was the truth. I certainly wasn't going to tell her about my plan to hurry through my dad's frustrating *Carpe Diem* list so I could buy the bakery. Spotting a fork under a table, I bent down and picked it up then put it in the dirty silverware bin. "I worked here for a few years in college, so I told Bernie I'd fill in as manager."

"You're just 'filling in' as a manager? Must be nice." Her tone was suddenly laced with sarcasm, which irritated me. Although, I supposed my casual approach to managing the bakery could come across as a bit snooty to someone working as a barista.

"What's *your* story?" I asked. Normally, I wouldn't pry into someone's private life. But Avery had felt fine prying into mine so I figured it was fair play. I fully expected her to clam up and give me one of those "back off" looks.

Instead, she shrugged, and said a little wistfully,

"You know the drill. Bad relationship. Even worse break-up. Now I'm starting over in a new city. Yada yada."

"Wow." Not the most revealing answer, but I was kind of surprised she'd opened up to me at all. Women only opened up to me . . . well, pretty much never. Except for Mary Ann the other night, who'd opened up to me big-time. Was something in the air? "I'm sorry to hear about all of that, but change can be good."

Unless it's the kind of change that forces you complete an entire list of tasks that make poking your eye out with a marshmallow stick sound preferable. Ugh. Why did I have to think about the word "marshmallow" when those deliciously tempting marshmallow fudge bars were only a few steps away?

Maybe they were all gone. I certainly was *not* going to check.

"Interesting." Avery's voice held her signature humorous tone.

My gaze snapped over to her. "What's interesting?"

She glanced up at the clock on the wall, then leaned against the broom handle she was holding. "That look on your face. I'm dying to know what you were thinking.

Care to share?"

Normally my answer would be a firm "no." But I'd been holding in all of the day's events, so I found myself taking a deep breath. "My dad died when I was fourteen. This morning, my mom gave me a letter from him containing a *Carpe Diem* list he wants me to complete. I'm not looking forward to completing the tasks, but I don't have a choice."

She swept the broom across the floor in short pushes even though I remembered her sweeping that area about fifteen minutes ago. "What's on the list?" she asked.

My stomach knotted. "For one, host a girls' night, which sounds like torture."

"That's kind of an odd thing for a dad to ask." She squatted down, then swept a few specks of dirt into the dust pan. "But what's the problem? Invite some people over."

I sighed, humiliated by what I was about to admit. "I'm afraid nobody would show up. I wasn't exactly popular at my last job."

"That doesn't surprise me." She suddenly froze, then glanced over at me, seeming to notice that my jaw had pretty much hit the floor. "Sorry. That totally slipped out. But you had to know that about yourself, right? I mean, look at you. No hair out of place, size four I'm guessing, and you've got to be glossing off and on all day in the bathroom because nobody's lip shine lasts that long. Anyway, women tend to find that kind of perfection intimidating."

I blinked in shock, wondering if that could be true. "When I was young, girls used to call me 'Marshmallow Melinda' because I'd been kind of pudgy. I'm committed to leaving that nickname far behind forever."

"Mission achieved." She emptied the specks of dirt from the dustpan into the garbage then glanced at the clock on the wall again, making me wonder if she was in a hurry to leave. "Girls can be cruel. I won't even get into all of the names I was called when I was in grade school. You can't let mean people keep you down."

"I know." My brows furrowed as I ran my rag over the last dirty table. "But it's not like I've had any luck with friends as an adult, either. Thus, my problem with hosting a girls' night."

"I'll come to your girls' night," she said, as if it were

no big deal. "Name the time and place. What kind of drinks are you going to be serving?"

"You'd really come?" I bit my lip, surprised that she was interested in hanging out with me. She probably just felt bad because I'd complained about completing my dad's list. For most, hanging with the girls was no big thing. For me, this would be an epic hurdle to jump over. Feeling nervous, I inhaled slowly. "How about Friday night? I can serve champagne to celebrate crossing one of the tasks off my dad's *Carpe Diem* list."

She let out a laugh, then checked her watch. "*Carpe Diem*? I can't wait to hear what else he put on a list with that kind of name."

I frowned, wondering why she was checking the time yet again.

As if on cue, the *ding-a-ling* of a bell chimed. My gaze flew to the now-opened front door, and in stepped Nate Carter. He wore dark pants, his black leather jacket, and held a white-handled paper bag in his hand. What was he doing here? It was well after five and the bakery was closed.

"It's about time you got here." Avery strode toward

him, and set the broom against the wall. "There's only so many times I can sweep the same area."

"Sorry, I'm late. There was a long line for pick-up orders." He turned to me, and his mouth curved upward. "Hope you're hungry for Italian."

Avery leaned over the front counter so far her body was hanging over, showing off the rhinestone crosses on the back pockets of her jeans. She retrieved her handbag, then slid off the counter and made her way to the front door. "Looking forward to the girls' night, Melinda. See you guys tomorrow."

"Wait . . ." I called out as she slipped through the door, which swung shut behind her, leaving me alone in the bakery with the very sexy boy-next-door who'd crushed me. I turned to him. "Did you have Avery stall me after the bakery closed?"

He turned the lock on the back of the door. "Only because I remembered Café Mattia is your favorite restaurant, and it's all the way across town. I thought I'd be here sooner, so I had to recruit reinforcements."

"To ambush me," I pointed out. Holding the wet rag in one hand, I put the other on my hip. "Normally one *invites* someone to have dinner with them."

The corner of his mouth lifted. "I did and you turned me down, remember? Can we discuss this upstairs? I don't want our dinner to get cold. I assume angel hair pasta marinara is still your favorite?" He turned and started up the stairs that led to the private rooftop terrace. Then he glanced back over his shoulder. "Come on, Melinda. One meal with an old friend. What's that going to hurt?"

It could hurt plenty. Just like that one kiss years ago that had ripped me apart. But I reminded myself that I wasn't that same young girl anymore. I was a strong adult, who had worked in this bakery and resisted those tempting chocolate marshmallow fudge bars. So I could certainly resist the equally enticing Nate Carter.

Chapter Four

I followed Nate up the stairs until we reached the top of Bernie's two-story building, then I stopped and looked around. The private rooftop terrace had a three and a half foot railing surrounding the tiled space, with various plants scattered around the edges. Under the dark evening sky, I glanced out at the surrounding rooftops, admiring the bird's eye view of this charming neighborhood.

This outdoor space felt so special that it seemed like a shame Bernie had never used the terrace as part of his business. When we were in junior high, Nate and I used to sneak up here with his friends while his dad was working downstairs. When it was late enough in the evening the boys would tell ghost stories, which had always freaked me out.

Thinking of the multitude of memories, a smile formed on my lips. It had been years since I'd been up here—or maybe since anyone had been up here, judging by the dead leaves and grime. This place could really use some T.L.C. Glancing around, I pictured a few improvements I could do, then immediately envisioned hosting elegant parties up here once I owned the bakery. Perhaps an exclusive Saturday night dinner where guests had to purchase tickets in advance. The concept excited me.

Suddenly I pictured groups of ladies dressed up enjoying my Saturday night parties with their friends, and something tugged at my heart. I thought I'd gotten over longing to be included in a group of friends that seemed so easy for most women. Maybe the "forced" girls' night this Friday was putting the spotlight on the fact that I'd always be an outsider.

I sighed. At least I would love my job.

In order to buy Bernie's Bakery, though, I had to get through the four tasks on my dad's *Carpe Diem* list pronto before someone else put an offer on the building. The girls' night was already in the works for Friday night. I'd also texted Ginger earlier to see if she'd allow me to have a dog at her condo—the local shelter was full of poor pups needing a home, right? Now I was waiting to hear back. I'd run out to the shelter as soon as Ginger gave me the green light.

That left me two more tasks to work on. Only date someone who leaves you breathless, and fix your biggest regret.

The last guy I'd dated was a successful financial analyst—my mom clearly shouldn't have married so adventurous, so I stuck with cautious business men who don't go riding off into the sunset on wild mustangs then break their necks halfway down the trail—and although he had sounded good on paper, he hadn't come anywhere close to leaving me breathless.

And fix my biggest regret? That would prove problematic since it meant going up in a hot air balloon with my dad and he was dead. I'd wanted to say "yes" to him each and every time he'd invited me, but I'd been scared. Now it was too late.

Why had my dad given me such difficult tasks? Instead of helping me seize life, they were starting to seize me a headache.

Needing to get this dinner over with so I could work on my dreaded list, I turned in the direction Nate had gone when we'd arrived up here. Next to one of the railings sat a white-clothed table with two candles in the center that he'd apparently set up. There was also a bottle of wine on a nearby cart.

Nate stopped next to the table, set the white paper bag with our dinner on the cart, then pulled a lighter from his pocket. I frowned as he lit the candles.

This "friendly" rooftop meal looked *way* too romantic. Also, it was pretty nervy of him to secretly arrange this dinner after the way he'd left things between us when he'd moved away. I needed to keep it crystal clear that this meal was in no way an actual date. In truth, we weren't really even friends since he'd ended that relationship by never calling me again.

Pivoting back toward the hatch we'd come through, I flipped on the light switch, illuminating the neglected terrace. I nodded. "Much better."

Nate twisted my way as I strolled toward the table. "What gives?"

"Dim lighting reminds me too much of a date." I draped my blazer over the back of a chair, set my purse on the floor beside it, then turned to him. My heart tugged at his disappointed expression. "You and I don't need candlelight to eat a meal together. I'm actually confused as to why you're going to all of this trouble to have dinner with me, anyway."

His eyes flicked to mine. "Maybe I've missed you."

My belly fluttered at his words, but I steeled my gaze. "That makes no sense. You moved away fourteen years ago without so much as a word to me. Now you appear out of nowhere and want to pick up our friendship where we left off? What would be the point of that? You'll probably take off when you're dad's feeling better, then I'll never hear from you again."

"I can see why you'd think that." His jaw tightened and he focused on popping the cork out of the wine bottle. Then he poured burgundy liquid into two glasses, and handed one of them to me. "But you have no idea how hard it was on me to make the decision to move to Paris."

I took a sip, then huffed a little. "I understand that was difficult. But you still could've called to say you were moving."

"No, I couldn't." His voice was firm, and his eyes flickered with emotion. "If I'd seen you, or spoken with you, then I wouldn't have been able to leave." He shook his head, and blew out a breath. "I needed to cut ties so I could go with my mom. She needed me."

My mouth opened slightly, but I was momentarily speechless as his words hung heavily in the air. All this time I thought he hadn't cared enough. Now he was saying the exact opposite was true. He'd cared so much, and that was the *reason* he hadn't called me. Oh, the irony.

I pressed my fingertips to my temple, rubbing the growing tension there, then finally tossed my hand up in frustration. "You could've at least written to me at some point."

"Yeah, I should have." He stepped toward me, brushing his fingers over mine, sending tingles up my arm. He studied my face, as if taking me all in for the first time. Then he bent down, his jade-green eyes locking with mine. "But I was a stupid kid who had messed up. I was afraid you wouldn't forgive me."

"You didn't give me the chance to," I shot back, thinking of all the nights I'd spent wishing he would call me, wondering if I'd ever hear from him again.

"You have the chance now." He lifted my hand,

caressing my palm with his thumb. "I can't rewind time to go back and fix my mistakes. But I can show you I've changed, if you'll let me."

I glanced away, focusing on a twinkling light in the sky that was either a planet or a star. As much as he'd hurt me, I couldn't imagine the pain he'd gone through when his parents divorced, especially with him having to move to a foreign country and away from his dad. I should've gotten his number from Bernie and called him. We'd been best friends for years growing up, and I'd let my stupid feelings for him get in the way. I wouldn't make that mistake again.

I turned back to him, and raised my shoulders. "All right. Let's move forward. I mean, you did remember my favorite restaurant."

His tense expression relaxed. Then he stepped forward, surprising me by wrapping his arms around my waist and lifting me off the ground. His mouth brushed my ear, sending goose bumps down my neck. "I really did miss you."

"I missed you, too." Even though I should've pulled away, I hugged him back, and it felt *totally* different than when we were kids. He'd been handsome before, but he'd been a boy—tall and lanky. Now, he'd become a man, and had completely filled out. His upper back felt strong and firm beneath my grip, tempting me to remove his jacket so I could run my hands over his taut muscles without the thick leather in the way.

A stream of flutters rolled through my belly, causing me to go on red alert. I stepped back. "So, it's agreed. We're friends, and you'll never disappear on me again."

Although friends should *not* want to trace every hard line of the other friend's body. My attraction to him was obvious—not to mention totally understandable, considering his off-the-charts level of hotness. But I needed to keep my feelings in check so I wouldn't lose him again. I lifted my lashes and found him peering down at me.

His green eyes simmered. "I won't let you down this time."

Gulp. I needed to lighten things up. "Then feed me. I'm starving."

"I can take care of that." He smiled, then busied himself transferring the food from the containers to the plates. In under a minute, a delicious-looking Italian dinner was on the table, and he slipped into the seat across from me. "How did it go today with your dad's letter?"

I sipped my wine, then set the glass down. "Let's just say, I've found new meaning to the word *bittersweet*."

"How so?" He lifted his own glass and leaned back in his chair.

I twirled my fork tines in the angel hair pasta, shaking my head in thought. "My dad died so suddenly, we weren't able to say good-bye to him."

His brows came together. "I heard the hot air balloon crashed into power lines. And there were no survivors. That's awful."

"Yes." I nodded, the phantom feelings from that terrible day making my heart squeeze. But talking about it with Nate made it a little easier. With him, I didn't have to be the strong daughter, the one who watched helplessly while my mom painted one ceramic hot air balloon after another. "My dad loved going up in those hot air balloons. He actually asked for his ashes to be sprinkled over the Sierras from one. My mom is trying to hire someone to do it, but she's having trouble finding a company who will because of laws and stuff."

His expression changed for a moment, and he seemed to study the plate in front of him. Then his gaze focused on me again. "What did his letter to you say?"

I swallowed a bite of pasta. "A sweet good-bye. Then, in true Dad fashion, he gave me homework."

He let out an incredulous laugh. "You're joking."

"Oh, no." I waved a finger, then reached for my wine glass. "He assigned me a *Carpe Diem* list, and told my mom that I can't have my inheritance until it's completed."

"He wants you to seize the day, huh?" Nate asked, then popped a forkful of pasta into his mouth. He chewed slowly, studying me as I shrugged. He leaned forward, holding out his palm. "Let me see this list."

I reached into my purse, removed the envelope, and handed it to him.

He pulled out the letter and read silently to himself. Then he cleared his throat. "Rescue a dog. Host a girls' night. Only date someone who leaves you breathless. Fix your biggest regret."

Scrunching up my face, I twirled some more pasta onto my fork. "I should probably consider myself lucky there are only four tasks on his list, and that they could all technically take place in the country. But my biggest problem is how quickly I have to complete them."

His forehead wrinkled. "He's been gone since you were fourteen. Why are you suddenly in a rush?"

I swallowed my last bite of food, then set my fork down. I wanted to tell Nate about my new dream, but I was afraid of saying it aloud. "I can't tell you."

He paused while reaching for the wine bottle. "Why not?"

"It's a secret." I waited for him to refill my glass, then I lifted it by the stem, and stood. I nodded my head in the direction of the railing across the terrace, then we strolled over there side by side.

When I stopped at the railing, I stared at the scattered neighborhood lights. Nate came up beside me, his arm nudging mine. Then he leaned close to my ear and whispered, "If you don't share your secret with me, I'm going to tell you the scariest ghost story of your life."

His breath tickled the sensitive spot on my neck, and

I shivered. "Fine. But you'd have to promise not to tell your dad, or anyone."

He leaned onto the metal bar of the railing, then tilted his head my way. "I promise."

A nervous flutter ran through me, and I bit my lip. "I want to buy Bernie's Bakery. I found the asking price online, and my inheritance money will just cover it."

"You want to buy the bakery," he repeated, his expression filled with surprise. "Why don't you tell my dad you're interested? I'm sure he'd be willing to take it off the market until you complete your list."

"No." I took a long sip of wine, then shook my head adamantly. "I know he would hold off selling, but then he'd be doing what's in my best interest and not his. He's sick and needs to retire. I won't cause him an ounce more stress when his health is in jeopardy. I'll complete the list fast . . . somehow."

His eyes peered into mine, then the corner of his mouth curved upward. "I'm going to help you."

I laughed at his determined expression. "Really?"

"Absolutely." He dangled his wrists over the railing, still gripping my dad's letter in his hand. "That's what friends are for, right?"

My heart warmed. "I've never had much luck with friends."

"Well, your luck's changing, starting today." From beneath my dad's letter, he revealed a small square package wrapped in wax paper. "You know what else a friend does?" He unfolded the corners of the wax paper slowly. Next he peeled the paper back revealing a rectangular fudge bar that I recognized all too well. "After picking up your favorite dinner, a friend makes sure you have your favorite dessert."

I stared at the chocolate marshmallow fudge bar, inhaling the sweet scent. My mouth watered, but I shook my head. "I gave those up years ago."

He broke off a small piece and popped it into his mouth. Then he closed his eyes and made a humming sound. "Why would you *ever* do such a thing?"

Squeezing my wine stem, I licked my bottom lip. "They weren't good for me."

"Hmm." His breath smelled like fudge, making it— and *him*—hard to resist. "What if they weren't good for you before, but they are now?" he asked.

"I'm doing fine without them in my life." My thoughts swirled, wondering if we were talking about the fudge bars or Nate. Either way, I had to stay strong. "I need to focus on buying the bakery, and I'm under a deadline."

"Right. You need to complete the *Carpe Diem* list quickly." He slowly put another bite of fudge between his enticingly full lips. I watched him chew leisurely as if he were deliberately savoring the taste to tease me. "Let's talk about task number three," he said.

My gaze darted from his mouth to his eyes, trying to get my mind off the delicious flavor on his tongue right now. "Number three . . ." I squinted, thinking about the order of the list, then my eyes widened when I realized the third task. "Only date someone who leaves you breathless."

He nodded, his gaze pinning me in place. "Are you dating anyone right now?"

"I just stopped seeing someone, actually." Despite my resolve to keep a friendly distance from Nate, my heart had a mind of its own and its steady beat kicked up to a trot, pounding against my ribcage. We *so* needed to talk about a different task on the *Carpe Diem* list. Any other task would be good right about now. "It's better to complete tasks in order. I sent a text to my roommate earlier asking if it's okay to have a dog in the condo. She has two kittens so I'm hoping she won't have a problem with a little canine hair mixed in."

Oh, man. I needed to stop rambling. Had I ever been so nervous in my life?

Looking amazingly focused, he leaned closer to me, until his mouth was only inches away from mine. "Did you break up with that guy because he didn't leave you breathless?" His voice was a low rumble and his fingers grazed along my jawline, leaving a trail of heat where his skin had touched. "Because I'm sure no man would have the strength to leave you on his own will," he whispered.

He fingered a strand of hair that had fallen against my face, causing all of the air to leave my chest. I gripped the railing for support and my gaze dropped to his mouth, which was right there just waiting for me to press my lips against his. A sense of déjà vu washed over me. Like we'd been here before, with his mouth just a breath away from mine. And we had. My first kiss, which had been *amazing. . . .*

Tension mounted inside me, and an insistent voice inside me screamed *kiss him. Kiss him.* I leaned forward slightly, sliding my tongue over my bottom lip, trying to recall why this was a bad idea. I inhaled to calm myself, but got a whiff of that sweet marshmallow fudge bar instead. The temptation to taste him was overwhelming, embracing me like the most wicked kind of torture.

My head became fuzzy and my resolve began to dissipate.

"Give me the fudge." I whispered the demand, as if pleading for mercy. My heart thudded in my chest. Maybe if I indulged in a little something sweet, my craving to taste him would go away.

The corner of his mouth curved upward. "I'd hoped you'd change your mind."

But instead of placing the fudge bar on the palm I held out, he broke off a piece and held it to my mouth. I couldn't resist anymore. Locking my gaze on his, I parted my lips, then drew the sugary fudge into my mouth.

Indescribable sweetness exploded against my tongue, reminding me of everything I'd loved in my youth.

Running through the park. Throwing the tennis ball to my loveable pooch, Checkers. Jumping into my dad's arms. Kissing Nate on the swing.

Our gaze held as he pushed the last of the fudge bite into my mouth. My tongue swiped the edge of his finger, causing more-than-friendly zings to zap my belly. Suddenly, my déjà vu turned into my déjà date, and I was ready to taste more than fudge.

"We can't do this." I whispered, but I couldn't make my legs retreat.

"Sure we can." Without taking his eyes off mine, he took my wine glass from me, setting it next to his on the edge of a planter box. Then he slipped his arms around me, pulled me close to him, and held me there. "Do you have any idea how many times I've wanted to hold you since I left? Since *before* I left?"

A shiver ran through me. I couldn't believe he'd had feelings for me when we were young. I'd been *so* in love with him. But that was I was fourteen, carefree, and never thought about the future. "This is not a good idea."

"You're right." He bent toward me, brushing his mouth over mine, back and forth, until a small sound escaped me. "It's a *great* idea."

I couldn't argue with that logic when his mouth captured mine, leaving me completely breathless but wanting more. He kissed me over and over, sending me spinning somewhere between the past and the present—in a déjà dream I couldn't escape from even if I wanted to, which I didn't.

My hands glided across his firm chest, over his shoulders, then I laced them through the back of his thick hair, pulling him closer. His tongue claimed mine repeatedly. He tasted of fudge and Nate, which was a perfect combination. I savored each kiss, never wanting them to end. Then a light breeze blew my hair back, snapping me out of my decadent haze.

I tasted him one more time before I pulled back, then fought to catch my breath as I stepped away. His hands immediately found mine, and he pulled me back to him. "Where do you think you're going? I just found you again. I'm not going to let you escape."

How was it possible that I was even more attracted to Nate after all of these years? Had to be hormones or something, because I wanted to *carpe diem* with Nate right here on the terrace. This was so *not* the distance I was supposed to be keeping.

"Thank you for dinner. But I really need to go home and work on my list."

The corner of his mouth rose and he pressed his mouth to mine. "I thought we were working on number three."

I took a deep breath to gather my strength, then I wriggled out of his arms. "I can't date you, Nate."

"Why not?" He frowned when I picked up my wine glass and strode toward the table, but he quickly caught up to me. "If I didn't leave you breathless, I'm happy to try again."

I tossed him a "don't even think about it" look. "You plied me with marshmallow fudge bar, which is so not fair. I lost my head for a moment. That's all that happened."

"Your dad knew what was good for you. That's why he put number three on that list."

I set my empty glass on the table a little too hard. "My dad should've been more detailed with number three. Attraction is all well and good. But I need to date someone who's stable. Not someone who's going to fall off a cliff or get eaten by a shark while he's at work."

He grinned, lifting my jacket from the back of my chair. "You saw the Bali photos on my website? I just uploaded them this afternoon."

My cheeks heated as I slipped my arms into my jacket and chastised myself for not having more self-control when it came to my cell phone's Internet service. "I'm glad you have a job you love. That's what I'm going for, too. But I can't cross something off the *Carpe Diem* list if I haven't truly completed it." I grabbed my purse from the ground and slipped it over my shoulder. "And you and I are not dating."

"You'll change your mind." He grinned, holding out my dad's letter. "Just like the fudge."

"Don't count on it." I snatched the letter from his hand, then slipped through the hatch, feeling completely flustered as I hurried down the stairs.

I didn't care what number three on my dad's *Carpe Diem* list said, dating someone who left me breathless was *not* enough. I needed someone who would be around in fifty years, not a wanderlust like Nate who might get eaten by a grizzly bear while hiking in the Rocky Mountains.

Unfortunately, reminding myself about that didn't make leaving Nate any easier.

Chapter Five

The next day I spent over thirteen hours straight working at Bernie's Bakery, making everything from chocolate croissants to custard pies. I took inventory, placed supply orders, and even served customers while Avery was on her lunch break. But instead of being worn out by such a long day, I felt invigorated.

Managing the bakery felt completely different from my customer service job in the software industry, which would have wiped me out after such a full day. I *loved* baking in the early hours, helping the customers, and organizing the business side. Today just reinforced that buying Bernie's Bakery was essential to my future happiness.

I'd almost cried when Bernie's Realtor, Wendy Watts, put up the "for sale" sign outside the bakery this morning, and it was all I could do not to rip it down and yell, "It's *mine.*"

At least, it would be mine as soon as I got my inheritance money, which was why I was attacking the first task on my dad's *Carpe Diem* list tonight.

Ginger had given me two thumbs up this morning for getting a dog as long as it was less than twenty-five pounds, which was the homeowners association's rule. She'd also mentioned that her friend, Sarah Carlton, ran a dog rescue service out of her house. So I made a six o'clock appointment with Sarah to adopt one of her rescues. I'd give the dog a nice home, but I'd keep my feelings tucked safely away from him.

No creature could ever replace Checkers.

I arrived home from the bakery after five o'clock, which didn't give me much time to eat before heading over to Sarah's house, let alone time to wash the flour out of my hair. Nate had appeared in the bakery's kitchen at five a.m., insisting that friends help friends bake. When I'd protested, he'd merely flicked flour in my direction, and we'd ended up having a bit of showdown involving multiple spices.

Nate had won, so I ended up letting him help me bake—customers were arriving soon after all. But I'd held my own in the spice fight and he'd left that afternoon smelling of cinnamon, nutmeg, and sugar.

Yum. His scent had been even more delicious, but I managed to resist him, which hadn't been easy. The man looked *hot* wearing an apron, and despite my need to distance myself from him, he'd made me laugh over and over like old times.

Now, at home, I practically inhaled my dinner so I wouldn't be late. Then I set my plate in the dishwasher, grabbed my keys off the counter, and was heading for the door when Mary Ann arrived unexpectedly. She insisted on coming with me to Sarah's house, and I took her up on her offer to drive since my hands were shaking.

The drive was only a few miles, but I couldn't remember any of it. I'd chewed on my thumbnail the entire ride, knowing I'd never be able to open my heart up to another dog like I had with my beloved Checkers. If only my dad had given me some other task since this one just reminded me of the sweet companion I'd lost, causing stabbing pain through my chest.

"What's going on, Melinda?" Mary Ann pulled into the right side of Sarah's driveway, and pushed her gearshift into park. "Spill, so I don't have to start guessing."

"What makes you think anything's going on?" I opened the door, gave her my most innocent look, then jumped out of the car before she could respond.

Mary Ann's blond head popped out of the driver's side. "I asked about the hot guy from the bakery several times, but you've totally ignored me." She pushed her driver's side door shut. "Plus, you're suddenly adopting a dog? Animal hair drives you *nuts*. I mean, really. You flinch any time Gilligan or The Professor rub against your ankle."

I normally smiled at the mention of my roommate Ginger's cats' names. It was hilarious how she and Mary Ann totally had the *Gilligan's Island* thing going on. But my nerves were too raw right now. I was about to adopt a dog, and all I could think about was the ripping pain I'd felt when Checkers had died. I'd need to keep emotional distance from this new dog. That's all there was to it.

"See? You're doing it again, ignoring me. And you're wearing the same expression I had when my facialist moved to Tahiti with her boyfriend. Not exactly the look of someone excited to bring home a pooch. Am I wrong?" She raised her brow as we traipsed up Sarah's front walkway.

At the doorstep, I turned to Mary Ann, whose eyes grew large with concern. I sighed. Here she was, once again, reaching out to me. Part of me wanted to tell her how my dog died when I was fourteen and how that had crushed me. That my dad had died soon after and the idea of losing someone else I loved gave me this deep dark sinking feeling in the pit of my stomach.

But I'd learned to keep a heavily guarded wall around my heart, and it forced me to hold back. Although I longed to open up to the bubbly blonde who spoke everything on her mind, and to the adventurous rebel who rode a motorcycle (oops—I promised myself I wouldn't think of Nate tonight), the thought made me feel entirely too vulnerable.

So I turned to Mary Ann as I pressed the doorbell, wishing I could be more like her and just say everything that was on my mind. I decided to try the short version for a start. "My dad died when I was fourteen, and my mom just found a letter he'd written to me in his will—"

"I'm so sorry." She reached out, threw her arms around me, and squeezed. "How awful. I had no idea."

I froze, momentarily stunned at how easily she was able to let her feelings fly. I patted her back awkwardly. "Thanks, Mary Ann. That's . . . very sweet of you."

The front door opened with a squeak. "Are you guys all right?" a female voice asked.

I quickly turned to smile at the pretty woman with silky brown hair who looked about my age, dressed in dog-hair covered sweats and a warm smile.

"Melinda's dad died when she was fourteen, and her mom *just* found a letter he'd written to her." Mary Ann sniffed, then dabbed the corners of her eyes. "Melinda, this is Sarah. Sarah, Melinda."

Sarah's smile grew even wider. "Nice to meet you, Melinda. I'm very sorry to hear about your dad. How surreal to get a letter from him after all of this time."

"You don't know the half of it," I blurted, unexpectedly.

Mary Ann kept her gaze on me as she stepped inside the entryway, and Sarah closed the door behind us. "Was it hard for you to read it?" Mary Ann asked.

"Yes." I pressed my lips together and followed her inside, thinking it would've been easier if I had asked

Nate to stay with me like I'd wanted. Even though it had been years since we'd seen each other, being with him felt comforting—like we were still best friends.

"What did he say in his letter? If you don't mind my asking . . ." Sarah's tone was friendly, but cautious.

I gave her a reassuring smile, touched by how genuinely interested she seemed. "He told me good-bye and that he'd always love me."

"Oh!" Mary Ann's eyes watered. "Sounds like your dad was really special. Mine wouldn't write me a letter in a million years, let alone say he loves me. I'm just fortunate he completed rehab. We're having a celebratory dinner Saturday night and I'm so *not* looking forward to seeing him."

I gave Mary Ann a sympathetic look. "My dad wasn't perfect, by any means. In his letter, he also left me a *Carpe Diem* list, which I have to complete."

"Seize the day?" Sarah asked.

I nodded, following her down the hall. "Task one is to adopt a dog."

"Oh!" Mary Ann's hand flew to her mouth as she skipped along beside me. "That makes total sense now.

You're adopting the dog because your dad wanted you to, which is *so* sweet. Was he an animal lover?"

We crossed through the living room, went out the sliding back door, then entered Sarah's yard. Barking ensued.

"I don't know," I mumbled. My dad liked animals well enough, but that's not why he'd put the task on my list. He knew how much I loved Checkers and he wanted me to seize the day—whatever *that* meant. Sigh.

"These are the rescues available for adoption." Sarah wore a wistful smile as she leaned on the chain link fence of her dog run. There were eight dogs inside, most of whom were jumping against the fence and barking loudly.

Thinking of Checkers, my heart pinched. I glanced away from the yippers, mentally grumbling to my dad about how he could do this to me. What if my roommate rethought her decision to let me have a dog once she heard the barking in her tranquil condo? I wasn't really a cat person, but Ginger's kittens were certainly quiet. And, even more, I'd made sure not to bond with them.

For a moment, I pondered the possibility of my mom

letting me modify task number one to a cat. No, that was just wishful thinking. My mom and dad had been sticklers for backing each other up, so I'd have to complete task one as he wrote it if I wanted the inheritance money so I could buy the bakery.

"I rescued that one from the pound." Sarah interrupted my thoughts by pointing to a yellow lab mix. "He's sweet, but rambunctious for sure." Then she waved her finger at a tiny brown fluffy dog. "A woman dropped that one off after she found her wandering the streets." Her lips pressed together as she faced me. "Is there a certain type of personality you're looking for in a pet?"

"Low maintenance." I came up next to Sarah, keeping my gaze away from the dogs, prolonging the inevitable decision as long as I could. "Potty-trained. Obedient. Under twenty-five pounds. And not too needy. I'm giving him a home, but we're both going to need our own space."

"You'll want one of the older dogs then." Sarah lifted the latch on the gate. "Why don't you go inside and get to know them? You can give them a few commands to see which will be the best fit for you."

"Can I go inside, too?" Mary Ann squealed with delight when Sarah nodded. She squeezed through the narrow gap Sarah had cracked open, then she was promptly attacked by obsessive licks from random dogs.

While the pups were diverted, I slipped inside, and went to the opposite end of the pen so I could study each dog from afar to evaluate which would be the most self-sufficient. As soon as I sat down in the corner by myself, a little brown dog with a long back trotted over, and started jumping on me.

"Down, doggy. *Down*," I said, sternly. But the pup ignored my commands, and continued to lick my face, arms, and any spot it could get its wet tongue on. Then it stopped suddenly and started hacking.

Hagh! Hagh!

"You don't want that one." Sarah's brows came together. "Definitely high maintenance. I rescued her from the pound yesterday, and I'm pretty sure she has kennel cough." She shook her head. "It's likely she'll need antibiotics. Plus, I noticed flakes of skin all over her coat, which could be from malnourishment. I'll have to take her to the vet, which I'm guessing will be a hefty bill."

Hagh! Hagh! The short wiener dog arched her chin forward as she coughed again, choking as if she might keel over at any second. Then she stopped abruptly, quieted, and paused as if waiting for her coughing fit to continue. When it didn't, she shook her head, ears flapping about her. Then her dark-eyed gaze met mine and she began jumping on me with vigor, attacking me with her wet tongue.

"Sit! Sit!" I instructed, but it was no use. The dog continued to assault me with her energetic licks and she couldn't get close enough. I leaned away, pressing my back against the metal fence, but she wiggled onto my lap and began sniffing under my arms. "Stop!"

"Come over here, Melinda!" Mary Ann called out from across the dog run. "I've found the perfect dog for you! He such a good boy."

Blocking my face from the crazy hot dog invading my personal space, I turned in time to see Mary Ann point to the ground.

She circled her finger in the air. "Roll over. Now . . . *sit*."

The pretty black dog with the shiny coat followed her commands, then sat quietly at attention waiting for the next instruction.

"Isn't he great?" Mary Ann called out. "Come check him out."

I fought to push to my feet, but the little brown pup—which had to be some kind of dachshund mix—pounced on me. Her obviously too-long nails scratched my arms, and when I managed to wring myself free, my sleeves had snags. "Oh, no!"

"I'll come get her from you," Sarah said, apparently sensing my distress.

As I heard the metal gate squeak open, I used both of my hands to hold the squirmy little dog down. But the chaotic wiener dog wiggled erratically, struggling to get free so she could no doubt find a spot of me to slobber on.

"Come here, girl." Sarah lifted her away from me, holding the pup in the crook of her elbow, and the chaos stopped.

I fought to catch my breath now that the struggle was over, and for some reason I glanced up. A dark-brown gaze met mine, staring at me wide-eyed, with a look of longing. Then something happened. The seal around my heart cracked, slipping away like hot liquid, leaving a long forgotten spot exposed.

I reached toward her. "Wait . . ."

Sarah swiveled. With a look of confusion, she placed the wiener dog into my outstretched arms, and quietly stepped away.

"Hi, girl," I said, holding her against me.

She whimpered with joy, scrambling up my chest with her two front paws as if she couldn't get close enough to me. Her wet nose brushed my chin and she began licking my cheek repeatedly, her tail swooping back and forth behind her.

"What do you think?" I asked, staring into her brown eyes. With a shaky hand, I rubbed behind her ears, and she pushed her nose into my palm, finding a new licking spot. And in that one little nudge, my heart melted, and there was no more fighting it.

I knew she was mine.

****

On Wednesday morning Bernie's Realtor, Wendy

Watts, dropped in to say she had an interested buyer coming to tour the bakery and building on Friday, and my heart pretty much stopped. As Wendy rattled on about the importance of having everything in perfect order for the showing, a wave of dizziness overtook me. I gripped the counter for support.

I needed to go see my mom as soon as possible and beg for more time to complete my dad's *Carpe Diem* list. But due to my (still unnamed) pup's intermittent hacking, I first had to first take her to the check-up appointment I'd made at All Things Furry—the vet clinic where my roommate took her cats.

The vet had come highly recommended by Ginger's friend, Ellen Holbrook, who also happened to be an old co-worker of mine. Although Ellen and I had both worked in the same department for years, I was practically the only woman at the company who hadn't been invited to her wedding—or later, to her baby shower.

This was of the many reasons I groaned when Mary Ann called as I was leaving the vet's office, and asked if she could invite Ellen to my girls' night on Friday.

"Ellen's baby is due any day now and she's been cooped up in her house since she's been on maternity leave," Mary Ann pleaded, emphatically. "A spa night with the girls is just what she needs."

"Spa night?" I blinked, setting my little pooch on the front passenger seat, along with the bag of expensive medications I'd had to charge on my credit card (yep, kennel cough). When I released my pooch she immediately scrambled toward the front passenger's side window, propping herself up on her hind paws so she could press her nose against the window and study the two kids running through the parking lot.

Ruff! Ruff!

"Yeah, doesn't a spa night sound fun?" Mary Ann's voice bellowed enthusiasm. "You've had an emotional week, and I think it would be good for you."

Apparently she thought it would be good for Ellen Holbrook, too. I was already feeling like an outsider at my first girls' night ever. Thanks, Dad.

I sucked in a breath. "Honestly, I don't think Ellen would want to come to a party I'm hosting." I connected Mary Ann to my car's speakerphone, then set my cell down so I had both hands free. "I'm pretty sure she doesn't like me," I said, hoping she'd tell me I was being paranoid.

Long pause. "Okay, that's another reason I'm suggesting the spa night. It's come to my attention that Ellen and some of the other gals find you a little intimidating."

"Me?" I'd been backing out of the parking space and braked way too hard when she'd called me intimidating, remembering that Avery had said the exact same thing to me the other day. "What do you mean?"

"Oh, you *know*." Her voice rang out cheerfully. "How you're always so put together, and look like you just stepped out of a fashion magazine. Personally, I say more power to you. But apparently some people find it off-putting. Surprised me, too."

"I appreciate your honesty." I slammed my foot on the gas, making the car lurch forward before I sped down the street. I'd worked with some of those women at the office for over four years, and had always thought I'd done something wrong to make them not like me. But it was my appearance? I pressed my lips together. "In grade school, I was made fun of for being an ugly duckling. Now, nobody likes me because I look *too* good?"

"It's not that they don't like you," she said, quickly. Then she sighed. "Don't get mad at me for saying this, but you are kind of hard to get to know. I mean, every time I want to hang out with you I pretty much have to invite myself."

"When have you had to . . .?" My brows came together as I thought back to when we'd gone out to dinner last weekend, to breakfast at the bakery on Monday, and then to get my (nameless) dog last night. She'd initiated each invitation. Shoot, *she'd* even called *me* just now. I shook my head, and sighed. "You're totally right. I guess I have trouble reaching out."

"It's no biggie. I just think Ellen might have an easier time getting to know you in a relaxed environment like a spa night." She lowered her voice. "It's hard to be intimidated by someone who's wearing a facial masque. Know what I'm saying?"

A tiny laugh escaped as I realized, ironically, how hard Mary Ann was trying to include me in the group, even though I was resisting emphatically. I slowed my car to make a right turn, realizing that somewhere along the way Mary Ann had become my friend.

My eyes blurred and I blinked back the tears. I pulled into mom's driveway, swiping under my eyes as I came to a stop. "A spa night is a great idea and I appreciate you thinking of me. Please do invite Ellen. I . . . hope she comes."

Mary Ann let out a whoop. "Excellent. We're going to have a lot of fun. I'd better go now. I have a hot date with someone new."

I laughed, because it seemed like Mary Ann only dated a guy once or twice, before she moved on to the next one. "Have fun, and don't break his heart."

Speaking of broken hearts, my mind immediately raced to Nate. Even though I promised myself to keep things with him on the "friends" level, something still echoed inside me that he might disappear again. But he seemed sincere in his promise, so I should try to trust him again.

Besides, I had enough on my plate right now. Convincing my mom to front my inheritance money would be no easy feat, but I had to try.

Ruff! Ruff!

My little hot dog's tail whipped back and forth rapidly and my gaze followed hers. The front door of my mom's house opened and my mom walked out with a younger guy with a fabulous physique. What the . . .?

That's when I noticed the motorcycle parked ahead of me in the driveway. Nate. What in the world was he doing here?

Chapter Six

Sitting behind the wheel of my car, I stared at Nate and my mom who were deep in conversation on her tiny front porch. They didn't seem to notice me parked in the driveway, and I wondered what they could possibly be talking about so intently. Had Nate dropped by just to say hi to her? Had he come by to see me? Although, that made no sense since I didn't live here anymore.

Whatever the reason, Nate's being here was problematic for two reasons. First, I needed to beg and plead that my mom advance me my inheritance, since those potential buyers were coming to the bakery on Friday, and I couldn't very well do that with Nate (or any other witness) standing nearby. And second, Nate stood facing my mom at the front door, giving me way too good a view of his backside, which caused my belly to go up in flames.

I'm sorry, but it really should be against the law for him to wear jeans that snug. How did he expect me to stay "just friends" with him when he looked that hot? It was so *not* my fault that I wanted to slide my hands over every inch of him and feel his rippling muscles. My mind immediately flashed to our delicious kisses the other night, leaving me wanting a repeat right here, and right now. . . .

Focus, Melinda. Focus!

I shook my head, knowing I could *not* lose Bernie's Bakery. Customer service work would make me even more miserable now that I'd tasted what it was like to be at my dream job.

Mentally pumping myself up to convince my mom to advance the money, I got out of the car, walking my wiener dog along beside me using the leash Sarah had loaned me until I had the time to buy—make that *charge* on my credit card—a collar and leash of my own.

Ruff! Ruff!

My four-legged hot dog raced toward the porch, yanking so hard on the leash that her collar tightened around her neck and she started gasping. Not that this slowed her down at all. Despite what had to be a terribly uncomfortable position, she continued thrusting forward until she came close enough to jump obsessively on

Nate's pant leg.

Ruff! Ruff!

Without flinching, he stared down at my little yipper with his gorgeous jade-green eyes framed with long dark lashes—ah, I remember when I had a calmer less complicated life—then his gaze caught mine as I approached. "Hey, Melinda." His eyes lit up. "Does this belong to you?"

"Yes, she does." I smiled proudly, my gaze dropping to where my pooch was sniffing Nate's boot. "Her main hobby seems to be licking whatever she can get her tongue on, though, so consider yourself warned."

He knelt down beside my little pup, and started scratching both sides of her long neck with his fingers. "What's her name?"

"Haven't picked one yet." I watched Nate get all affectionate with my dog, and his actions only ignited the flame in my belly. He really needed to stop before I started getting affectionate with *him*. "I just picked her up from a dog rescue last night."

"Sweetheart, you finally got another dog." My mom's mouth spread into a wide smile, and she brought both of her hands to her chest, twisting her pearls. "That's wonderful."

"It's also task number one on Dad's *Carpe Diem* list," I said, giving her a meaningful look. In addition to wanting to know what Nate was doing here, I really needed my mom to listen to reason regarding my inheritance. "We need to talk that list. Um, alone."

Still rubbing his hands over my pup, Nate tilted his head up, squinting. "That a hint for me to take off?"

"Well, I—" I was in mid-sentence when the neighbor's tabby cat, Muffy, suddenly darted across the porch, letting out a loud *Meowrr!* when she caught sight of my pup.

Apparently Muffy was more enticing to my new pooch than Nate was, because she chased the cat unexpectedly, yanking her leash out of my grip.

"Hey!" I shouted as the end of the leash followed my hyper pup, who dashed after Muffy. I watched in shock as my wiener dog disappeared down the sidewalk at full speed, her browns ears flopping up and down. "Come back, girl!"

She ignored me, of course.

I gripped the sides of my head, starting to panic. "What if she runs into the street and gets hit by a car?"

"I'm on it." Nate's voice sounded heroic to my ears as he darted after my galloping hot dog, his muscular legs pounding up and down against the pavement in true super hero fashion.

"This is a disaster!" I cried out, glancing quickly at my mom's wide-eyed expression before I dropped my purse and keys to hurry after them. As I pumped my arms as fast as I could, I found myself wishing I hadn't worn heels today. Each painful *clomp* against the cemented walk had me rethinking dressing like I'd stepped out of a magazine.

Forget that other women found my appearance intimidating, dressing up was just not practical when your disobedient dog took off randomly after the neighbor's cat with no regard to her safety or my feet—not to mention my feet had already been aching after standing in heels for thirteen hours at the bakery yesterday and six hours so far today.

I rounded the corner, glancing up and down the street, but nobody was in sight. Not the cat, the dog, or Nate.

My heart squeezed. Where had they gone? Taking off my shoes, I trotted to the end of the block, then scanned my surroundings. Across the street at my favorite park, I spotted them. My wiener dog had literally treed the cat, and Nate now had a hold of my crazy dog's leash.

As I made my way across the street, Nate led my pup over to the swing set. He sat in my favorite swing, while my pup dug her nose in the sand beneath him. Then her ears pricked up as I approached, and she trotted over to me, wagging her tail.

Relieved that she was safe, I squatted down next to her, cupping her face in my hands. "Don't you *ever* do that to me again."

In answer, she nudged her nose in my palm and began licking there. I let out a breath, waiting for all of the tension to ease out of me. It didn't. Now that my dog was safe, I still had my mom to deal with. And Nate. I glanced over at the swing.

The corner of his mouth turned up. "Looks like I'm a handy guy to have around, after all. Wouldn't you say?"

"In this case, I would most definitely agree." I smiled, then tied the leash around the beam, watching my pup sniffing at a rock in the sand. Then I eased onto the other swing, gripping a chain with each hand. "Why *were* you at my mom's house, anyway?"

"You mentioned that your dad wanted his ashes sprinkled over the Sierras from a hot air balloon. Well, I found a friend of a friend who's willing to take me up and look the other way while I carry out your dad's wishes. Your mom and I decided this Sunday would work best."

Of course Nate would know someone rebellious who was willing to break the rules. I sighed. Then a cold chill rolled through me as I realized what that meant. My throat tightened. "Today's Wednesday. So that means in a few days the last remains of my dad will be gone."

He reached over, and caressed my cheek. "I'm sorry. I can't imagine how hard that must be. I hope you don't mind that I offered to help. I really liked your dad, and felt bad that your mom was having trouble carrying out his final wish."

My eyes burned. "He had a lot of last wishes," I said quietly. Then I shook my head, thinking about his *Carpe Diem* list—especially task number four. I glanced over at Nate who was watching me intently, and I sucked in a breath. "In my dad's letter, he said I had to fix my biggest regret . . ."

"I remember." He lifted my hand from where I'd gripped the chain, then laced his fingers through mine, stroking the groove between my thumb and index finger. His jade-green eyes darkened with emotion. "Anything I can do to help?"

"Thanks for offering, but there's nothing anyone can do to help." A bitter laugh escaped. Then my gaze blurred and a boulder formed in my throat. "My biggest regret is that I never went up in a hot air balloon with my dad. It's what he loved doing most in the world. He was even thinking about starting a tour business. Did you know that?"

The corners of his mouth turned downward and he shook his head.

"He absolutely loved being up there." I glanced up at the baby-blue sky, fighting to hold my tears in. "He kept inviting me to join him, but I'm scared of heights. So I always turned him down. The night before the accident, he'd asked me to go up with him the next day and I'd *wanted* to say yes. But I didn't."

A horrified expression crossed Nate's handsome features, and his hand tightened around mine. "I'm glad you didn't go that day."

I stared off in the distance, knowing it was no use begging my mom for the inheritance until I'd at least lined up all four tasks. "My biggest regret is that I didn't go up in the hot air balloon ride with him, and that's something I can't fix now that he's gone. I'll never be able to complete his *Carpe Diem* list."

"That's not exactly true." He stared at me intently, his Adam's apple bobbing up and down. "You have one last chance on Sunday when I take your dad up for his final ride."

Chills vibrated through me, along with a tingle of hope. "But he's dead. . . And those are only his ashes. He won't know I'm up there with him."

"Maybe he will and maybe he won't. But you'll know. Won't you?"

I bit my lip, wondering if there was any possibility my dad would be aware I went up with him—that I'd finally been brave. "Um, when I said that I'm scared of heights that was kind of an understatement. Petrified is probably a more accurate word."

Slipping off his seat, he came around in front of my swing. "You can do it, princess."

Tingles flittered across my chest at the nickname my dad had always called me.

"I'll be with you the entire time." His tone made it sound like a stroll in the park instead of my greatest fear realized. Then he proceeded to grip both edges of my seat, his hands brushing against my hips.

Ignoring the flitters in my belly, I raised my brow. "You'll stay with me even if I'm hyperventilating and clawing into you with my nails?"

"Even then." He pushed me up high in front of him like he'd done that last day when we were fourteen. The edges of his mouth curled. "Nothing can scare me away from you ever again."

"Nothing?" I whispered as a traitorous ripple of excitement ran through me, sparking another sense of déjà vu. I had been fourteen. Nate had lifted me high in the swing and held me there, suspended with anticipation before he leaned forward and kissed me.

Then he'd disappeared.

Remembering why I needed to keep my distance from him, I slid off the seat, wiggled under his arm, and went to get my dog. The bakery was my primary focus and this pointless flirtation with Nate was distracting me.

Instantly, he caught my elbow then swung me back around so I was facing him. "Where do you think you're going?"

"Just leaving." I tried not to concentrate on how close he was standing to me, or on the way his shirt stretched across his muscular chest, giving me the irrational urge to slide my hands over him. I avoided his gaze, afraid he'd be able to read my thoughts. "I have to find a way to buy the bakery before it's too late. Potential buyers are coming to look at the building on Friday."

"I know." He lifted my chin so my gaze met his. "But didn't we just solve that problem? If you go up in the hot air balloon with me on Sunday, then you'll have completed the list and can have your inheritance money to buy the bakery."

I shook my head. "I'll only have completed three of the tasks. I still haven't dated someone who leaves me breathless."

"Now that sounds like an invitation." Suddenly, he pulled me into his arms, then, with his arm securely around me, he dipped me as if we were dancing—so low that I felt the ends of my hair skim along the sand. The air rushed out of my chest and I stared into jade-green eyes framed by dark lashes, wondering if he was going to kiss me. I found myself hoping he would.

He leaned closer until his mouth was barely a millimeter away. "Do you, or do you not, feel breathless?" he whispered.

I gasped for air. "This . . . is *not* a date," I managed to get out.

"I'll give you that." He swooped me upright, then grinned. "But the other night was a date. I brought you dinner on the rooftop, and a lovely bottle of Bordeaux. There was also candlelight, which you ruined by turning on the rooftop lights. But the candles were still there burning. Dinner, plus wine, plus candlelight, plus *kissing*, equals a date."

"You and I are *not* dating," I said, despite the fact that he'd almost just kissed me and I was dying to make him kiss me for real. An invisible tug pulled me to him and it took all of my strength to resist.

Nate held a hand up. "We'll argue about our relationship status another time. And I'll win. But if you'd just let me call my dad, I'm sure he'd take the bakery off—"

"No," I said, firmly. "Bernie can't have any more stress. He has to make the decision that's best for him, not the one that's best for me."

He let out an exasperated breath. "You're being entirely too stubborn about that, but fine. At least talk to your mom. Tell her you'll have the *Carpe Diem* list completed on Sunday so she should release your inheritance funds early. Convince her."

"That's what I was trying to do earlier, when *someone* took off running after the neighbor's cat." I pointed an accusatory finger in the direction of my dog, who I noticed had dug a hole in the sand so deep she'd reached something dark and mucky that was now covering her snout as well as parts of her legs.

Ruff! Ruff!

Great. On top of everything else, now I needed to give my dog another bath.

I felt a pinch in the spot between my brows. "Why must she get into so much trouble? I swear that little brown hot dog is my love and my torment all rolled into one."

Nate smirked, then bent down to pet her, and she began energetically licking his arms. "I think she sweet."

My mouth twisted as his word echoed in my head. "You know what else is sweet, brown, and tortures me?"

His face brightened. "Me?"

"You're not brown," I answered, since he was technically correct in the other aspects. Then I smiled, thinking of those chocolate marshmallow treats that had seduced me again after fourteen years. "Fudge. It's the perfect name for her."

He lifted her up from under her arms, holding her out so she was peering straight at him, legs dangling. "Is your name Fudge?"

Ruff! Ruff! Her tail propelled back and forth so fast, I was afraid she might fall out of his grip.

"She likes that name." He set her down on the sand, holding the end of her leash tightly as she scampered toward the edge of the sandbox so fast she started choking herself on the collar again. He gave me a side-glance. "Now you'll have something to call her when she takes off again."

"Great." I shook my head, smirking, suddenly remembering all of the mischief Checkers had gotten into when I'd had him. He had actually eaten one of the plastic chips from my Checkers game, which was how he'd earned his name. "Let's go back to my mom's house, so I can throw myself at her mercy."

"It's a plan," Nate said, leading Fudge along next to him.

Together, the three of us left the park, heading for my mom's house. And when I glanced down at Fudge, for a moment I swear I saw the faint image of Checkers trotting happily beside her. Tongue hanging out of his mouth, he met my gaze with light in his eyes, then he veered in the opposite direction.

With tears in my eyes, I watched him continue running off in the distance, then he slowly faded away. I'd always miss him, but I was finally ready to let him go. And for the first time since that awful day so many years ago, even more than the pain of losing him . . . I remembered the love.

Chapter Seven

Although I had begged and pleaded to my mom on Wednesday, she refused to advance any of my inheritance funds until my dad's *Carpe Diem* list was completed. I was beyond frustrated with her.

I'd pointed out the very obvious fact that my dad had most likely assumed that I'd complete the *Carpe Diem* list by the time I turned eighteen, and that if my mom hadn't waited to open his letter then I would've had his list fourteen years ago—thus the list would be done already. In turn, she'd pointed out that I'd rejected the funds when I was eighteen and also several times thereafter. Then she had the nerve to tell me that I was lucky she hadn't given the money away liked I'd originally told her to.

Her very annoying point infuriated me since I couldn't exactly argue with her logic. Then she'd annoyingly proclaimed that everything happened for a reason. "What reason would be good enough for me to lose the bakery?" I'd shot back.

My mom's face had grown stern, like I hadn't seen since my dad had died. "You're missing the whole reason behind your dad's *Carpe Diem* list. The tasks are more important than the insurance money. Period."

"Easy for you to say when you're not the one who'll have to work in a job you hate!" I'd countered, then stormed off.

Needless to say, the exchange had *not* been pretty.

When Friday morning came, I tried to convince myself that everything with the bakery really would work out the way it was supposed to, but those thoughts immediately felt like a load of garbage. In the past week, I'd grown more attached to the bakery than ever, and I knew coming this close to my dream then losing it would devastate me. But I didn't know what else I could do.

I'd worn flats to work today, but I'd still done myself up "like I'd stepped out of a fashion magazine" as Mary Ann had put it. This time, though, I wasn't dressing up to lose my ugly duckling rep, or to cover up of any of my (many) insecurities. Although I wasn't sure how to make myself less intimidating, I liked my clothes and the way I looked so I wasn't making any changes—other than wearing more comfortable shoes since I'd be on my feet all day.

I'd also eaten an entire fudge bar yesterday, which had been *delish*.

Currently, I was behind the counter assisting Avery when the *ding-a-ling* of a bell chimed overhead. Wendy Watts sailed through the doorway with a grand smile, and with an older suited gentleman wearing a tight expression as if he'd eaten a sour apple. Here came my competition for Bernie's Bakery, and I wanted to cry.

"Good morning!" Wendy waved to Avery and me warmly as if she'd known us forever and we were the best of friends. Then she turned to her prospective buyer. "These are our happy workers." She'd used a singsong voice on "happy workers" as if the joyfulness of Avery and me could make his dreams come true (and bring her a fat commission, of course).

"She's good." Avery spoke in a hushed voice and gave me a look that said she was impressed by Wendy Watts, the queen of Realtors whose face appeared on billboards across the city and outside our door. "Remind me to use her if I'm ever in the position to buy something."

"Hrmmf . . ." I made a non-committal sound since I didn't want to believe in Wendy's ability to sell this place to anyone but me.

"As you know, the owner is selling the building and the bakery as a set." Wendy clasped her hands together, leaning toward her buyer as if she were revealing some kind of secret just for him. "If you didn't want to run the business yourself, it is self-sufficient. But once the sale closes, of course, the choice is yours with what you want to do with the space. There are so many possibilities and there's even a rooftop terrace."

My mind immediately shot to my dinner with Nate on the terrace Monday night, then a swarm of memories from my youth flooded my brain, causing a wave of nausea to invade me. What if this guy with the sour expression bought Bernie's Bakery and turned it into a cigar store? Or something else equally suited to his tight disposition?

Avery leaned toward me. "I hope Mr. Grumpy Face will keep the bakery running using his 'happy workers' or I'm hosed. Do you know how hard it is to find a job right now?"

Unfortunately, I did. I also knew what it felt like to be micro-millimeters from my dream and not know if it would rip right out from under me. I couldn't witness anymore.

I turned away. "I'll be in the back office if Wendy needs me, but hopefully she won't," I told Avery.

"Okay," she said, then addressed a customer who had just walked in.

My stomach roiled and I hurried to my office, wondering if a jar of antacids could reduce the boiling frenzy in my belly. I couldn't lose Bernie's Bakery to Mr. Sour Face just days before I completed my dad's *Carpe Diem* list. It would be the biggest form of injustice of all time. So would going back to temping.

Hoping a chow-down of antacids would take the edge off my anxiety, I opened the office door, then stopped short. Nate was sitting on the office couch, holding Fudge in his lap. And he did *not* look happy.

****

"What are you doing here?" I stared at Nate, hoping Bernie's health hadn't deteriorated suddenly. When I'd dropped by Bernie's house with a basket of bread yesterday morning, the dark circles under his eyes had faded and his skin color had returned to normal. "Is your dad all right?"

"For the moment." Nate's jaw was tight as he rose to his feet, then set Fudge on the sofa cushion. "But he's going to have a heart attack for real if he sells his bakery to that sour puss Wendy brought in, then finds out you were willing to buy his business the entire time."

"You know how I feel about talking to Bernie about that, so don't start on me right now." I strode to my desk, pulled open the top drawer, then fished through paper clips, sticky notes, and such, searching for any sign of antacids. There had to be at least a small packet with all of the sugar around here. Were two little tablets asking so much out of life?

"Princess, you're a wreck . . ." His expression shifted and his eyes filled with concern. Then he came toward the desk, and reached for me. "I'm worried about you. Come here."

I held my palm up, and continued searching through more drawers with the other hand. "Please keep a friend-worthy distance. I'm at the end of what I can handle right now."

The muscles on his jaw twisted. "You're being irrational about thinking you're doing what's best for my dad, and about *us*."

"No, I'm protecting Bernie. And myself, for that matter." I pulled open the last drawer, ready to cry at the pain in my belly. If there was any justice on earth, I'd find an antacid in here right now.

Nate stepped toward me. "Protecting yourself from what? Me?"

"Um, duh?" I barely glanced at him as I shoved the final drawer shut, plopped into my office chair, and admitted defeat in the world of antacids. I dropped my head in my hands, devastated that I had nothing to soothe my aching tummy. Or maybe it was more than that. . . "I just can't catch a break right now."

"I'm here for you." Nate's massaged the top of my head briefly, then I felt him jump up onto the desk before he tucked a piece of hair behind my ear. "I already told you I'm not going anywhere this time."

"Even if that's true, it's not enough. You and are too

different." My stomach tightened even more, sending the burning up my throat. I lifted my head, then gestured between him and me. "We are *not* the same. Look at what happened with your mom and Bernie. She's adventurous, he's not, and that didn't end so well."

"You're comparing us to my parents?" His brows came together as his green eyes flared down at me. "Yeah, my dad was only adventurous one day of his life, which was how they ended up with me. And they *shouldn't* have gotten married because of that," he said, his voice thick with emotion. "Obviously."

"You see?" I stood, facing him, feeling terrible for bringing up such a painful time in his life. But he needed to forget about us, because the temptation to give in to him was tearing me apart. "I'm sorry for bringing up your parents. But I need you to get that this, you and me, can't work out."

He slid off the desk so our bodies were touching, then he cupped my face in his hands. "You're forgetting one important factor. My parents didn't *love* each other."

Tingles radiated through my body as that one four-letter word rang through my head. Lifting my lashes, jade-green eyes peered back at me. "What are you saying?"

He skimmed his thumbs along my cheeks. "I'm saying, look at *your* parents."

"Exactly." I pressed my hands to his chest. "My mom used to stress out every time my dad went off on one of his adventures. She'd worried he wouldn't come back, and the last time he didn't."

Nate's green eyes steeled. "People are killed every day in car wrecks on the freeway, from illnesses . . . you name it."

"Yeah, but—"

"Your dad died from a terrible accident." He gripped my shoulders, staring at me intently, his eyes flashing. "But that *accident* was a fluke. Bad luck. And I'm not denying how awful that was." He sucked in a breath, and his tone softened. "But how many times had he gone up in a hot air balloon before that and been fine? How many times do people go up in them every day?"

My pulse raced and I shook my head, still fighting it. "My parents shouldn't have gotten married. They were too different," I said, voicing the same concerns I had about Nate and me. But when I said the words aloud, they didn't ring as true as they had in my head.

"If *my* parents had truly loved each other, they wouldn't have let some differences keep them apart." He dropped his forehead to mine, and closed his eyes a moment. Then he brushed his lips against my cheek. "*Your* parents were amazing together. That's what we'd be like."

My heart pounded in my ears. "How do you know?"

"Because I felt it the moment I saw you again." He brushed his fingers across my jawline, then gazed down at me with absolute sincerity. "I was still as in love with you as I had been when I was just a dumb kid."

Butterflies assaulted my tummy and I swayed, my legs threatening to give out beneath me. "Y-You were in love with me?"

Strong arms looped around my waist, keeping me from falling over. "Wasn't it obvious?" he whispered.

"Um, *no*." I had to laugh at the irony, which tasted bittersweet. "I fought *my* feelings for *you* all those years, because I thought you only saw me as a friend."

The corners of his mouth turned upward. "Don't you

think it's way past time we stopped being stupid?"

I smiled up at this adventurous man, who'd had my heart before the very first time he'd kissed me. In answer to his question, I leaned forward and pressed my mouth to his, giving him everything in my heart that I'd been holding in way too long.

His mouth immediately claimed mine. Darts shot through my belly as his tongue nudged between my lips and I opened for him. His arms tightened around me and my hands smoothed over his muscular shoulders, as we tasted each other eagerly.

As our kisses deepened, I felt Fudge squeeze between us, pawing at my ankle as if she wanted to be part of the love. Then, a rush of adrenaline coursed through me, and, for a moment, I felt what it could be like to have everything I wanted.

My mom had said that everything happened for a reason. I'd finish my dad's *Carpe Diem* list on Sunday, and for the first time I felt hopeful she'd be right.

Chapter Eight

I was about to host my first girls' night ever, and I had no idea why my dad had thought this would be a good thing. Like I wasn't stressed out enough right now. Not only had Bernie's Realtor brought a potential buyer to tour the building this morning, she'd called this afternoon to inform me there was *second* buyer scheduled to look at the bakery tomorrow.

I'd seriously wanted to scream.

Instead I had spent the last two hours decorating for a spa night theme, clenching my teeth so hard that my jaw hurt. Yeah, the lights were dimmed low, numerous lit candles were scattered around the living room, and I'd put wind chime music on the stereo, but I was the exact opposite of relaxed. I had no time to attempt to chill out either.

Mary Ann, Ellen, and Avery would be here any minute. Earlier, Avery told me she was bringing a special surprise for me, and the gleam she'd had in her eye made me very nervous. My roommate, Ginger, had just gotten home from work—she's an interior decorator who'd had a job today in my mom's neighborhood—and was changing clothes in her room.

All I wanted to do was curl into the fetal position in bed, and beg the universe to throw me a bone for once in my life by letting me buy Bernie's Bakery. Was that really asking so much from life? I didn't think so. Instead, I had to play hostess to a group of women I wanted badly to be friends with but was scared wouldn't like me once they got to know my many imperfections.

I glanced around the living room, my gaze jumping from the foot spas Ginger had borrowed from her friends, to the paraffin bath, to assorted nail polishes, then to tubes of facial masques lined up on the coffee table. I liked being pampered as much as the next girl, but it seemed emotionally safer to focus on getting my inheritance money than risking my feelings for the chance to make real friendships.

It killed me how close I was to completing my dad's *Carpe Diem* list, and I could practically feel the pen between my fingers signing the closing documents to buy Bernie's building. I mean, really. I'd adopted a dog, I was dating someone who left me oh-so-breathless, and I was hosting a girls' night. All I had left was to force myself into that hot air balloon on Sunday, despite the massive fear creeping up my throat just thinking about it. Then I could get my inheritance first thing Monday morning.

I'd had my mom double-check the balance of my pending inheritance funds and the amount was just enough to cover Bernie's full asking price. Due to his health condition, he'd priced to sell right away, so I wouldn't even try to negotiate a lower price. Three more days, and the bakery would be mine. I just needed to hope neither of those buyers would be interested. *And* that I could survive my girls' night.

I put on velour sweats, a tee shirt with a bling heart (for good luck), and clipped my blond hair up in a twist. Checking my watch, I saw it was six o'clock on the dot, so I decided to pop the champagne and get a head start. I very obviously could use a drink. What if nobody showed up? My nerves frazzled even more. I trudged toward the refrigerator, then happened to glance at the dining table where I'd set up a myriad of decadent delights baked by *moi—*

My eyes bulged as I stopped in my tracks and gaped at the table. Standing on top of the dining table was my sweet little hot dog, Fudge. One of her four paws stood directly in the middle of a piece of carrot cake with cream cheese frosting, and she was currently eating the last of the quiches. I gasped. Her head snapped up as I slowly approached and instead of looking the slightest bit guilty, she started wagging her tail.

"No! Fudge, how *could* you?" I ran to the table, but it was too late. She'd either eaten or ruined every last snack. This was going to be one hungry crowd, because it's not like I had back-up appetizers. Who made back-up appetizers? Someone with a dog like mine, apparently. I swooped Fudge off the table, set her on the floor, then jabbed my index finger in her direction. "That was *not* nice! Not nice at all!"

She proceeded to jump up on her hind legs and attempt to lick my finger. Not exactly the look of regret and understanding I'd been hoping for.

Ginger burst into the kitchen, wearing her running shorts and a tee shirt. Her long dark hair was up in a ponytail. "I heard yelling. What's going on?"

I threw my hands out. "Fudge ate our hors d'oeuvres."

Ginger grimaced. "Oh, no. Anything I can do to help?"

The doorbell rang at the same time my cell phone beeped, so I gestured in the direction of the door. "Could you get that for me?"

"Of course." She sent me a sympathetic smile, then scooted out of the room.

I picked up my cell phone. There were two missed calls from Nate, and a text message from him, too. I ran my fingers over the screen to open the text: *I need to talk to you. It's important.*

My fingers flew over the keyboard, and I sent back: Fudge just ate all of the hors d'oeuvres for my party, and I'm freaking out. Can we talk tomorrow instead?

I glared at Fudge who was licking frosting off her paw. "How could you do this to me and then have the nerve to sit there looking so freaking cute?"

My cell phone beeped in my hand, and I checked the screen: Hang tight. New appetizers will be hand-delivered shortly. And we need to talk tonight.

A warm feeling washed over me since Nate was rescuing me yet again. First my dog who'd run after the cat, now my girls' night. He was going to deserve a medal soon. Or a kiss. Or ten kisses. . . .

I texted back: *Thank you SO much. Really.*

Moments later, my phone beeped: *Anytime, princess. See you shortly.*

My belly fluttered since he'd again used the nickname my dad had dubbed me. I could get very attached to him calling me that. Maybe it was because we'd been best friends growing up or something, but although we'd only just started dating, my heart already felt fully invested in Nate, which was both exciting and scary at the same time.

"Let's get this party started!" Avery danced into the kitchen with Ginger following behind her, then she pulled several items out of her red patent leather tote bag. "Lookie what I brought."

My first guest had arrived, which left me speechless. Well, technically she was the second guest since Ginger lived here. I couldn't believe this was happening that girl friends wanted to come hang out with me. It seemed unreal and part of me wanted to hide in the other room in case they somehow realized they'd made a mistake by coming and bolted. Me? Insecure? Maybe just a *lot*.

Swallowing the lump in my throat, my gaze dropped to the bottles in Avery's hand. "What are those for?"

She gestured to the purple streaks in her shoulder-length hair, which she wore pulled back at the bakery but had styled down tonight. "I catch you staring at my hair all the time. Don't you dare deny you do."

My immediate reaction was to protest. But Avery would just pin me down anyway, so I went to the fridge and shrugged. "It's such a beautiful color." I opened the refrigerator door and pulled out a bottle of champagne, hoping a (very full) glass would calm my nerves. "I can't figure out how you keep the streaks so vibrant."

"I dye it every week." She used a tone that said she thought everyone would know that was how you retained the color. "As you will also have to or believe me, the color will fade. Oh, did I mention the surprise I promised you tonight? We're dying a lock of your hair purple. *Surprise!*"

I gaped at her happy grin. "I can't dye my hair

purple."

She held the bottles higher. "Why not? I have everything you need."

The doorbell rang again, so I glanced at my roommate.

Ginger raised a finger. "I'll get that. But first, I have to state for the record that a purple lock would look fabulous with your blond hair."

I couldn't believe they were ganging up on me! Even though the color of Avery's hair was beautiful, I couldn't dye my hair purple for a lot of reasons. Tons. Now I just needed to come up with one. . . .

"I'll think about it," I said, hoping I could stall her while I figured out what was holding me back. I really did have hair envy, but people would notice me if I had purple hair. They might even stare at the color like I'd done with Avery's. If they looked too closely they'd see my imperfections, so it was safer to keep under the radar.

Avery took the champagne flute I handed her. "Don't worry. A few of these and your fear will fly right out the window," she said.

"Fear?" I frowned, pouring a glass of champagne for

Ginger and whoever had knocked on the door. Avery was so off base. "I'm not afraid."

She raised a brow. "Then why won't you say yes?"

I stared at her pretty purple hair, wondering how she'd ever had the guts to dye so many streaks. But I was not as brave as she was, so I raised a shoulder. "It's just not . . . me."

"I'm not buying that excuse, but it's your choice." Avery took a sip of champagne, then eyed the dining room table strangely. "Uh, what happened there?"

"Don't ask, but also don't eat any of it," I said, then twisted around as my old co-worker Ellen Holbrook came into the room.

Ellen was a pretty woman, who looked like the typical girl next door. She had dirty-blond hair, green eyes, and a majorly protruding baby belly that made me wonder how she managed to say upright. She'd always been polite to me at the office when we'd worked together, but I'd never been included in her in-group social outings no matter how much I'd wanted to be. Seeing her here actually made me feel like an intruder at my own party, and I once again felt the urge to go hide in my room.

Her mouth turned upward in a polite smile. "Hi, Melinda. It's nice to see you."

"You, too." I forced an awkward smile, wondering if my nerves had ever been this frazzled before.

"Hellooo!" A cheerful voice rang out then Mary Ann burst into the room. She threw her arms around Ellen. "I'm so glad you made it! Look at how adorable you are." She patted Ellen's belly, then turned to me. "Hey, you." She hugged me next, wearing a big smile, then faced Avery. "You must be Avery. I'm Mary Ann. You probably don't remember me, but we met at Bernie's Bakery. I bought a chocolate croissant."

Avery nodded in approval. "You have good taste."

"Uh, oh. Do I want to ask what happened here?" Mary Ann gestured toward the dining table, then put her index finger to her chin. "Why do I have the feeling that cute little Fudge had something to do with this?"

"I'm so sorry." I raised both hands, feeling terrible that my guests didn't have goodies to snack on. I had to be the worse first-time hostess ever. "More hors d'oeuvres are on their way, though. I promise." I checked my watch as if to prove it, hoping Nate would arrive soon with replenishments.

"May I get you something to drink?" I asked Ellen, then my gaze flicked to Avery who was showing Mary Ann the purple dye she'd brought for my hair. A small pang shot through me as I realized how tempted I was to dye a lock of my hair purple, which I never would've considered a week ago. What was happening to me?

"A glass of water would be great. Thanks." Ellen set her handbag on the counter, then slid onto a barstool. She turned to watch the other gals walk into the living room, then focused back on me. "I heard that you're still looking for permanent work."

"I am." I pressed the glass against the ice dispenser on the fridge, thinking about how badly I wanted that permanent job to be owning and running Bernie's Bakery.

"I know of a position available if you're interested."

"Oh?" I moved the glass to the water dispenser, then turned over my shoulder to look at Ellen. "Where?"

"Woodward Systems Corporation, actually." She nodded at my surprised expression, then she ran a hand over her belly. "Henry and I've talked. . . His business is doing well enough that we don't *need* my income. So, I've decided I'm not going back to work after the baby's born. I'm going to be a stay-at-home mommy."

My gaze immediately fell to Ellen's super swollen belly. Out of nowhere, the image of me being pregnant popped into my brain. Then Nate's jade-green eyes appeared in my mind. He was smiling down at me, rubbing his hand over my big belly, while feeding me a bite of chocolate marshmallow fudge bar. My heart swelled, and a flutter rippled through me.

"I've already given Kaitlin my notice," Ellen added.

I blinked, jerking out of my absurd vision. I hadn't had a serious relationship since college so I'd never pictured myself as a mom. But, surprisingly, I found myself wanting to replay the vision in my head again. Instead I handed Ellen her glass of water and smiled at her. "I'm really happy for you."

"Thanks." She beamed, then took a sip of water. "I felt terrible when the company laid you and Ginger off. Apparently Rich has been cutting a lot of costs. Rumor has it he might be selling the company."

I leaned against the island countertop. "That's what I suspected, too."

Ellen pressed her lips together. "Anyway, I mentioned to Kaitlin that I'd be seeing you tonight. She's going to start advertising for the customer service position on Monday. If you're interested in having your old job back, Kaitlin said to shoot her an email this weekend and the position's yours."

"Wow." I ran a hand through my hair, wondering what Rich Woodward would think if I dyed part of my hair purple. I mean, if I owned the bakery then I'd be my own boss and wouldn't have to worry about what any superior would think. Not that I wanted to dye my hair purple. . . Or did I? "I'm stunned. I never thought I'd have the option to work there again."

Hair color aside, the thought of going back to my customer service position depressed me. I was *so* close to achieving my new dream I could taste it. I opened my mouth to tell her I wasn't interested—

"Well, Kaitlin said she'd love to have you," Ellen said.

Hearing those words tugged at my heart since I'd

wanted to be part of their in-crowd for so long. Although, hello? Realization settled in. It's not like Kaitlin wanted to hang out with *me*. She was probably hoping I'd return so they wouldn't have to train someone new. Sigh.

"Thanks for letting me know." My answer was vague, but talking to Ellen like this made me feel part of their crowd. I wanted to enjoy the moment for a little while longer.

My cell phone beeped. I picked it up off the counter, then glanced at the screen. A message from Nate, which read: *Just picked up the order from Café Mattia. Be there in a few minutes. Don't forget we need to talk.*

I frowned, wondering what he wanted to talk about. I quickly typed back: *Thanks. See you soon.*

"Now that's a serious look." Avery reappeared in the kitchen, holding out her glass. "I'm ready for a refill."

"Already?" I chuckled, then reached for the champagne bottle. I poured the bubbly liquid into her flute.

"What's with the line between your brows?" she asked.

"Oh, nothing." I shook my head, knowing I was

probably worried for no reason. "It's just that Nate's dropping off some appetizers for us, and he says he needs to talk to me. "I'm sure it's nothing."

"So he hasn't told you yet?" Avery grimaced.

Chills trickled down my spine. I glanced at Ellen, who mumbled an excuse then left the room. "Nate hasn't told me what?"

Avery's expression changed, making me wish I'd never asked the question. "He got a call today while he was in the bakery. Some magazine offered him a job in Peru for an article they're doing on Machu Picchu. They need him to start right away and he'd be living there for six months."

My heart dropped to the floor. "A-Are you sure?"

She raised her shoulders. "I honestly wasn't trying to eavesdrop. But it was during that lull after lunch, and he was talking pretty loudly. Like he was excited."

My eyes burned. Of course Nate would be excited. The job sounded like an ideal opportunity for him. But where did that leave me? Us?

Suddenly, the sound of the doorbell echoed across the condo. Nate.

Momentarily frozen, Avery and I exchanged a look. I blinked to keep tears at bay, but a boulder had formed in my throat. This was exactly why I should *not* have listened to my dad and dated someone who left me breathless. Nate was leaving me. Again.

Chapter Nine

I walked out of the kitchen on numb legs, heading to answer the front door. Avery trailed behind me into the living room. She sat on the sofa next to Mary Ann, wearing a worried expression so I looked away. My gaze traveled to Ginger and Ellen, whose feet were immersed in two foot spas as they chatted. All of my guests looked happy.

I, however, felt like the ground had crumbled beneath me.

I reached for the door handle, knowing Nate was on the other side with his dreaded news, and my hand froze. Then a hopeful thought flitted through my brain. Maybe when I opened the door this entire nightmare would go away. Maybe Nate would tell me that Avery had heard his phone conversation wrong. That there was no job offer in Peru, and he was not moving to South America.

Sucking in a deep breath, I gathered my strength, then opened the door. My breath caught in my throat as I stared up at Nate—not because he looked hot, which he *so* did. He wore his black leather jacket over a white shirt, and the colors made his jade-green eyes stand out even more. But I'd lost my breath because of the way his jaw tightened when he saw me. He had bad news. I could feel it.

"Hi." Tearing my gaze away from his intense look, I glanced at the bag he was holding. "Thanks for bringing over the appetizers. How much do I owe you?"

"Don't worry about it. I'm glad to help." He handed the bag to me, then gestured toward the front walkway. "Can we talk out here?"

"Sure," I said, even though no part of me wanted to have this talk. With a quick glance at Avery, I set the bag on the entry table, then pulled the door closed behind me. Nate had moved to the sidewalk by the street and my throat went dry as I dragged my feet over to him. "What's going on?"

I was beyond shocked that I'd been able to get out the question. I stopped just short of the sidewalk and braced myself for the answer that he was or wasn't moving to Peru. I held my breath.

His gaze pierced mine. "My dad got an offer on the

building and bakery."

"Um, what?" I blinked, sure I'd heard wrong.

"Wendy Watts called an hour ago." He started pacing back and forth. "Apparently she told the buyer from this morning that she had a showing tomorrow with another interested buyer, which is a great sales maneuver on her part. The pressure tactic worked too, because this morning's buyer submitted an all-cash offer for twenty percent over my dad's asking price."

"Twenty percent more?" My stomach dropped, but for a whole different reason than Nate leaving the country. Even if I had a couple more days to get my inheritance funds, which I obviously didn't, there was no possible way I could match that offer. I'd been close enough to my dream to taste the joy, but it had stayed just out of my reach. My shoulders slumped. "It's over then," I said, numbly.

"No, it's not." He stopped pacing, and faced me with a set stance. "I'm telling my dad you're buying the bakery and that you'll have the funds next week."

My hands balled into fists. "Absolutely not. You promised you wouldn't tell him."

His jaw muscles twitched and he threw his hand up in a frustrated gesture. "If one of us doesn't say something to my dad, then he'll accept the offer."

"Yes, but that price is way better than what I can pay. I've been offered my old job as a customer service rep, and I'm going to take it." My heart cracked as I said it, but I knew it was the best thing for Bernie. "This is your dad's retirement money. He's worked hard his whole life and he deserves the best price for his building and his business. I'm not going to guilt him into selling everything to me for less money."

"I can't just stand here and watch while you throw away—"

"You're not going to have to *watch* anything," I shot back, crossing my arms over my chest as adrenaline coursed through my veins. "You'll be in Peru. Won't you?"

His mouth opened slightly, then he tucked his chin. "How did you hear about that?"

"What does it matter?" Shaking my head, I moved around him to go back to the condo.

He stepped in front of me, blocking my path. "I

planned to discuss this with you, but I just received the offer this afternoon."

I tilted my head. "What's there to talk about?"

A hurt expression crossed his face. "Do you think I'm going to take a job in South America? I told you I'm here for good and I meant it."

My heart flipped in my chest. "So you turned down the offer then?" I watched the guilty look cross his face, and he avoided my gaze. I let out a slow breath. "If you're so set on staying in Sac, then why wouldn't you decline the job?"

He thrust a hand through his hair. "Look, it's not as easy as that. This is exactly the kind of opportunity I would've taken two weeks ago. And, yes, it was fun to think about for a day. But I'm not going." He reached for me, but I took a step back. His brows furrowed, and he kept his gaze intent on mine. "When I saw you again that was it for me. I'm not leaving you."

My eyes burned suddenly, and I turned away. "I-I can't think."

Hiking the Inca Trail in Peru. Visiting Machu Picchu. This was the Nate I knew, and also the man I loved. I would *never* want him to change. But I also didn't want to be the woman waiting at home for the dreaded phone call, telling me that a fun adventure had ended in a body bag. I couldn't bear that.

"You should take the job in Peru. That's who you are . . ." My mouth had moved, but I felt numb everywhere. Bile rose up my throat as I lifted my gaze to his. "I'm not cut out for this kind of life. I need someone who's more stable, who I know will return home each night."

"There are *no* guarantees in life." He bit the words out, the muscle in his jaw pulsing. "You have to seize each and every day, because we don't know what tomorrow will bring. Haven't we both learned that by now?" He lifted my hands, squeezing them between his own. "All of my travels have led me back here. The *only* adventure I want to take is spending the rest of my life with you."

My heart flipped. I wanted to believe what Nate was telling me, but then my chest tightened with doubt. I didn't know if someone like me belonged with someone as adventurous as him. He could get bored with me, and take off to live in another country just like his mom had done. Maybe Nate was right that his mom hadn't truly loved his dad, though. It was hard to know what to believe.

I *wanted* to be with Nate, but the likelihood of getting hurt seemed so incredibly huge it was beyond scary. So, just like when my dad had invited me up in the hot air balloon when I was young, I shook my head. "I'm sorry, but I can't do this." I squeezed his hands one more time before releasing them. "You belong with someone who'll rough it with you in Peru at a moment's notice. Not someone who will keep you from your dreams."

"Melinda—"

"No." My voice was firm and final. "We don't belong together."

"If you would just listen to me . . ."

I held my palm up to stop him from saying anything more. "This is for the best."

His breath caught in his throat, then his eyes darkened. "You're wrong about what you and I need. One day you might even realize that, but by then I'll be gone." He stared at me a moment, his cold look sending a chill down my spine. Then he stepped back. "Bye, princess."

"Good-bye, Nate." I held my breath as he walked away so I wouldn't fall apart. Closing my eyes, I heard his motorcycle rumble to life, then he sped off.

A stabbing pain speared my heart as I turned and wobbled back to my condo. All of the sorrow from my youth came rushing back to me, but as I'd done for many years I tried to convince myself I was fine. At least Nate and I had said good-bye to each other this time. At least I'd had a choice. But no matter how many ways I tried to spin it, the pain kept increasing at lightening speed, threatening to knock me over.

I made it to the front porch, but then a sharp pang struck my chest. I grabbed the doorjamb for support as the hurt and loss I'd ignored for the past fourteen years rushed at me. Bending over in physical pain, I clutched my hands to my chest as an animal-like sound escaped me.

I'd lost the bakery, and I'd lost Nate. I missed my dad so much, but why had he giving me his horrible *Carpe Diem* list? For so many years, I'd kept a tight seal around my heart in order to avoid the exact kind of unstoppable pain shooting through my chest right now. Another sob escaped as my face crumpled in defeat, and I'd never felt so hopeless.

So alone.

Then the front door opened, the squeaky hinges startling me. I glanced up to find Mary Ann and Avery staring down at me, their eyes large with concern. My immediate reaction was to hide or pretend everything was fine. But I didn't have time. Within moments, Mary Ann's arms came around me and she pulled me against her, murmuring all kinds of sweet things about how she was here for me.

Her compassionate words didn't change me losing my dad, or the bakery, or Nate, But as I cried into her shoulder the pain lifted just a little bit, knowing she cared about what I was going through and knowing I had friends to lean on.

Maybe a girls' night had been a good idea after all.

****

Early the next morning, I arrived at Bernie's Bakery feeling like a zombie, going through the motions on automatic baker-mode. After I'd cried for an embarrassing amount of time last night, I finally confided to the girls about what had happened. With Nate. The Bakery. The *Carpe Diem* list. Everything.

They'd listened attentively, then plied me with lavender oil and facial masques, sharing their own tragic break-up stories. Mary Ann even told us about the guy who'd broken her heart in college, prompting her to create her two-strikes-and-you're-out dating policy, which she felt I should implement immediately since she claimed life was too short to stick around for a third strike.

Her rules wouldn't have helped me with Nate, though. He and I were just too different.

I'd given in last night and let Avery dye a lock of my hair purple. I'd chosen the chunk behind my ear so the color would display nicely when I pulled half—or *all*—of my hair up, but I could easily hide it when I wore my hair down if I wasn't feeling so daring. The flash of color had almost made me smile when I'd put my hair up in a twist this morning, but I was still too depressed about losing the bakery.

I was even more devastated about losing Nate.

After I'd prepared all of the delicious delicacies at Bernie's Bakery, Wendy brought the second buyer to the bakery hoping she could top the first offer. Man, that woman was driven. The sight of the second buyer pinched my heart and I was beyond exhausted when my day at the bakery was over.

When I arrived home, Fudge greeted me at the door with a hundred licks. Then I strode into the kitchen and was surprised to find Mary Ann. She sat at the barstool with a plate of leftover angel hair pasta marinara in front of her. A fresh slice of pain stabbed my heart as I stared at my favorite pasta dish that Nate had brought over last night in addition to assorted appetizers. The coldness in his eyes flashed in my mind, and I shook my head to try to clear all thoughts of him.

"Hi," I said, fighting to ignore the green eyes that popped into my head again. I should definitely avoid the pasta marinara for dinner and have a sandwich instead. No bad memories in a turkey on rye. "What are you doing here?" I asked.

"Eating dinner," she said, her tone lacking its usual pep. Instead of eating like she claimed, though, she pushed the pasta around her plate with her fork.

"No, I meant . . . don't you have something going on tonight?" My brain cells tickled on the brink of remembering something she'd told me the night we'd picked up Fudge. I snapped my fingers. "I've got it. You're supposed to be at your dad's celebratory dinner for completing rehab. Isn't that where Ginger is?"

"Yeah." Mary Ann slumped onto her fist, glancing up at me. "But my sister believes our dad's truly in recovery. I'll feel like a fake if I go and pretend he's cured."

I leaned on the counter. "What do you mean?"

"My dad's been an alcoholic my entire life." She sat up, shoving the plate away from her. "Scotch has always been his priority. It's been one disappointment after another with him. This probably sounds terrible, but I'm just not interested in getting my feelings smashed again when he goes back to the bottle. You know?"

I gave her a sympathetic look. "I can understand how that would be scary."

Her eyes widened. "Am I being unreasonable?"

"No, I . . ." My words trailed off. I wanted to reassure her that she wasn't unreasonable, that she had every right to give up on her dad, but that wasn't how I felt. She didn't realize how lucky she was to still *have* her father, as imperfect as he might be. I'd give up anything in the whole world to have one more dinner with my dad.

She gripped my hand like she was grabbing a lifeline. "Please be honest with me, Melinda. What do you really think?"

I didn't want Mary Ann to make the same mistakes that I had made, but I had such a hard time opening up my feelings. I took a deep breath. "The last dinner I had with my dad was when I was fourteen." A lump formed in my throat as I remembered back to that night. "He asked me if I wanted to go for a hot balloon ride with him the next day."

Her hand squeezed mine, encouraging me to go on.

"I'd wanted to go up in a hot air balloon, but I was scared of heights, scared of getting hurt." The lump in my throat shifted into a boulder. "Now I'll never get another chance to take that ride with him, and there's nothing I can do to fix that." I looked at her meaningfully. "So let me ask you a question. If you miss supporting your dad with this dinner, miss giving him a second chance, will you regret your decision if something happens to him?"

Her delicate features suddenly tightened and her face reddened as she finally nodded. "Yes, I'd probably regret it for the rest of my life." A small sound escaped her. "But this is *so* hard . . ."

"I know." I pulled her into a hug, wishing I could ease some of her pain the way she'd done for me last night. "Life's *way* too hard sometimes. But I think the best way to fix a regret is not to make the mistake in the first place."

She sniffed then leaned away, wiping her nose. "What about you? You said Bernie's Realtor was showing the building to a second buyer today, right?"

I shook my head, confused at where she was going with this. "So?"

"If she's showing to a second buyer, then it's possible Bernie hasn't accepted the first offer yet. Twenty-four hours is a standard amount of time to respond in the business world, so there might still be a chance to let Bernie know you're interested."

My brows came together as I pulled a loaf of rye from the breadbox. "You're as bad as Nate."

"I'm just using your own logic." She held her hands up defensively. "Once the bakery sells, there's nothing you can do about it. I just think Bernie should have all of the facts before he makes his decision. Maybe the buyer is going to turn his bakery into a frozen yogurt shop and he'd rather accept a lower offer in order to keep his business alive."

A sharp pain sliced through my chest at the thought of a frozen yogurt shop replacing Bernie's Bakery. But there was nothing I could do about that now. "I emailed the human resources manager at my old job this morning to let her know I was interested in the customer service position that became available when Ellen gave her notice."

"But you didn't *like* working there," she reminded me.

"It's a steady job, and pays the bills." Even though I had a good paying job again to pay off my credit card, I'd never felt worse in my life. With a knot in my throat, I spread mustard over both pieces of bread, then I sliced through an onion with a vengeance. "Kaitlin already emailed me back and confirmed the job's mine. I start in a week, after I've fulfilled my promise to Bernie."

"You won't regret that decision? Or the decision you made about Nate?" She stared at me a few moments. When I didn't answer, she picked up her plate and set it in the sink. Then she checked her watch, and raised her brows. "I'm going to the dinner. Wish me luck."

"Good luck." I forced a smile, then watched her wave and disappear out of the kitchen. A moment later I heard the front door open and then close as she left.

I put the rest of my sandwich together, but I had no appetite. My mind whirled at our conversation, but talking to Bernie about the bakery was *not* the same as Mary Ann having dinner with her dad. Bernie wasn't my dad, but I was afraid he'd sacrifice his happiness for me anyway, and that wasn't right.

My cell phone beeped and I wondered if it was Mary Ann changing her mind. But when I checked my phone, my heart skipped a beat. It was a text from Nate: *Picking up your dad's ashes from your mom's at nine o'clock sharp tomorrow morning. So I'll pick you up at a quarter til?*

My heart pounded hard in my chest. What would be

the point of going up in the hot air balloon to scatter my dad's ashes? I didn't need to finish my dad's *Carpe Diem* list when I'd already lost the bakery. And my dad was dead. I'd turned him down and missed my chance to go up with him, which was just something I'd have to live with.

My fingers flew over my keyboard, and I typed back: I've decided not to go. Thanks for taking his ashes up, though. My mom really appreciates it.

Seconds later, my phone beeped again: Don't be ridiculous. I'll pick you up in the morning.

The thought of seeing Nate again before he left for Peru would literally feel like a dagger to the heart. So I typed back: *I'm not going. Please respect my decision.*

Having made my choice, I set my phone down, then started to put my sandwich makings away. It was time to get back to the calm life I'd had before Nate had reappeared and I'd learned that Bernie was selling his bakery. I'd work at Woodward Systems Corporation again, get my own place, and I'd only date men who wouldn't shatter my world.

Suddenly my cell phone beeped, startling me. I gaped

at another text from Nate. What could he possibly have left to say? Inhaling deeply, I ran my finger over the screen: *Your dad made his Carpe Diem list for you because he wanted you to seize life. Being alive isn't enough. You have to LIVE, too.*

Like the worst kind of masochist, I read his text over and over, especially the last line. *Being alive isn't enough. You have to LIVE, too.*

Squeezing the phone into my palm, I finally sank to the kitchen floor and sobbed. A wet nose nudged under my chin, licking several times until I opened my eyes. But when I gazed back at Fudge through my hot blurred vision, I saw that her tail wasn't wagging. Instead, she just stared at me with her brown eyes, and I couldn't help wondering if she was disappointed in me.

Chapter Ten

It had taken me forever to fall asleep, but I was still clutching my pillow when a *beeping* noise jolted me awake. I could feel Fudge's warm body cuddled by my feet under the covers, her rhythmic breathing going up and down against my ankle as my eyes adjusted to the darkness.

Beep! Beep!

A faint light shone from my nightstand and I realized my cell phone was going off. I lifted my cell, noting the time, which showed a couple minutes past ten in the evening. How long had I been asleep?

I remembered bawling my eyes out on the kitchen floor for an eternity until the sobs had subsided and exhaustion had won out. Then I'd somehow managed to climb into bed, although apparently I hadn't bothered to change out of my day clothes. Lovely.

My eyes felt swollen shut, and I could barely see through the narrow slits. I propped myself up on one elbow then ran my finger across the cell screen. There was a text from Mary Ann and I tapped on the image to open it.

Her text read: *Thank you so much for the talk earlier. This was the best dinner my family's had . . . well, pretty much ever. My life has been bittersweet. But I've been stuck in the bitter and not focusing on the sweet. Know what I mean?*

Since I was currently drenched in bitter, I knew exactly what she meant. I typed back: *So glad you had a good time. You deserve it.*

Then I plopped back down on my pillow, and did something very stupid. I re-read Nate's text from earlier: *Your dad made his Carpe Diem list because he wanted you to seize life. Being alive isn't enough. You have to LIVE, too.*

I moaned into my pillow. Nate's advice sounded all well and good in theory, but how many times could a person get knocked down before they didn't want to get up again?

His text infuriated me so much I wanted to take a chocolate marshmallow fudge bar and throw it at him. Unfortunately, the thought of fudge reminded me of Nate feeding me that sweet bite on the rooftop terrace, which then reminded me of my tongue swiping across his sugary-laced finger. A shiver ran through me.

Suddenly I was moaning into my pillow for an entirely different reason. I *missed* Nate. And it had only been a matter of hours since we'd broken up. How was I supposed to last a lifetime without him?

Reading his text one more time brought me to the conclusion that my phone was dangerous. All I wanted to do right now was text Nate and tell him to forget what I'd said about us being too different. Gripping the cell phone in my hand, my mind started floating. . . .

Moments later I stood in a hot air balloon, soaring across the sky on a sunny day. A beautiful jade-green bird flew by me, and I longed to feel its soft feathers. But as I reached toward its vibrant coat, the bird dipped beneath the basket. I leaned over the rim, stretching my hands out to touch it, but I lost my footing and tumbled over edge.

The air rushed out of my lungs as I fell at high speed, grasping desperately all around me but the only thing my hands latched onto was air. My stomach jumped into my throat and I gazed up at the hot air balloon above me as the bright yellow balloon shrank smaller and smaller the further I fell. What had I been thinking leaning over the edge? I'd wanted to ride in the basket, and with one stupid move I'd lost everything.

In the faint distance I heard a *beeping* sound. A rush of warmth washed over me, reminding me of Nate. Then my gaze shot beneath me. I plummeted toward the earth but my fear left me as the ground morphed into strong, muscular arms spread wide to catch me. I gasped, then glanced up at my savior. Jade-green eyes peered back at me. Nate.

The corners of his mouth turned upward. Without thinking, I kissed him. The warmth of his mouth on mine sent chills through every cell of my body. My arms tightened around his neck, but then he pulled away grinning. He gestured behind him to a brown horse with a white star above its eyes. In one fell swoop, he lifted me up and my leg straddled over the horse until I was sitting upright.

He mounted his own horse then we rode up the brown dirt path toward the cloud-covered peeks in the distance.

We were on an adventure *together* in Peru. Nate turned to me and smiled, filling my heart with more joy than I ever thought possible. Then I looked up, searching the sky until I found where it was brightest blue. The spot shifted as if someone was trying to tell me something.

Something *very* important that I couldn't decipher.

Suddenly, the sky darkened and a thunderous boom sounded, sending vibrations through my body. Lightening flashed through the sky, a bright streak illuminating the mountain peaks before darkness fell again. Then rain pelted down painfully hard. My gaze darted to where Nate had been riding next to me, but he wasn't there anymore.

I glanced behind me and there he was on the trail, and I was still riding off without him. He reached for me—

I bolted upright in bed, breathing rapidly. The sun shone through my blinds, and my face was soaked. I clasped my cheeks, swiping the wetness away on my long sleeves. I'd had a dream. No, make that a *nightmare*. And in an instant I knew what it all meant.

My falling from the sky wasn't from seizing life, it was me running from it. Bolting from the second chances

I'd been given with Nate, the bakery, and the hot air balloon. Oh, no! The hot air balloon! Nate was leaving my mom's house at nine o'clock.

I couldn't believe how I'd messed up on task four. I didn't need to finish the last task on the *Carpe Diem* list for the inheritance money, I had to finish it for my dad. For *me*.

My gaze shot to the clock on my nightstand and I noted it was ten minutes til nine o'clock. I grabbed my phone and dialed Nate's cell phone number. My heart thumped against my ribcage as I held my cell to my ear. "Pick up!"

The phone rang once, then went to voicemail. *This is Nate. You know what to do. . . .*

"No!" I redialed his number, but was sent straight to voicemail again. I threw my comforter off me and Fudge, then jumped from the bed. I raced to the kitchen and grabbed my keys and purse off the island counter.

"Good morning," Ginger said. I hadn't even noticed her at the dining table.

"I have to get to my mom's house before Nate goes up in the hot air balloon." I gasped frantically and watched her eyes widen as I checked the time on my cell. "And I only have eight minutes. Can you feed Fudge and let her out to potty?"

"Of course." She stood, following me as I ran to the front door. "Good luck!"

"Thanks!" I called out, dialing Nate again, but no dice. Voicemail. As I ran toward my car, I dialed my mom's phone number. It rang three times before the answering machine picked up. *Hi, you've reached Elizabeth. . . .* "Doesn't anyone answer their phone in an emergency?" I yelled.

I slid into the driver's seat, throwing my cell and handbag on the passenger seat next me, and started the car. I backed out of the parking space quickly, then zoomed toward my mom's house, hoping Nate would still be there. He had to be. He simply *had* to be.

****

As I drove to my mom's house, I couldn't believe how stupid I'd been. I'd told Mary Ann to seize her second chance with her dad, but I'd been too scared to do the same with Nate. In fact, I'd been too scared to take risks with the bakery, too; as soon as I'd been given the chance to get my old job back, I'd taken it.

When I reached a red light, I pulled up my Internet on my phone, and responded to the letter from Kaitlin with my voice recognition: *Kaitlin, Thank you so much for the opportunity to have my job back, but I have to turn it down. Hope to meet up with you socially sometime though. Best, Melinda*

It had taken major bravery to add that last part about hanging out, but after the compassionate support from my girls' night on Friday, I knew I needed to reach out to other people more even if it was difficult. Once I hit SEND on my email, the light turned green and I stepped on the gas. I would finish my dad's *Carpe Diem* list for me, and then I'd finally accept the inheritance funds he'd wanted me to have.

Although I couldn't take away from Bernie's retirement by telling him I wanted to buy his bakery, I could use the money to start my own bakery. Maybe I'd learn to love it as much as Bernie's Bakery one day. Melinda's Bakery? No, that sounded way lame. But I'd figure it out and pursue my dream. Yes, I would seize my second chances from now on!

It was two minutes after nine when I rounded the corner before my mom's house, and I just hoped that Nate was still there picking up my dad's ashes. I pulled into my mom's driveway at high speed, and a wave of relief passed through me when I spotted Nate's motorcycle parked beside the green lawn. I stopped my car just behind it, then dashed to the door.

I rang the doorbell. Then I tried the front door handle, which turned out to be unlocked, so I hurried inside. On the marble floor of the foyer were stacks of boxes with address labels on them. A couple of the boxes sat open, and some of my mom's ceramic hot air balloons peeked out. Weird.

"Nate!" I called out as I sped down the hall, passing the grandfather clock next to the staircase. My gaze darted to the family room where my dad's urn still sat, but nobody was in there. "Hello?"

I raced toward the kitchen, wondering where Nate and my mom could be. Then I stopped short when I spotted Bernie standing next to the granite kitchen countertop, wearing only a bathrobe. What the . . .?

Bernie's coffee mug froze halfway to his mouth.

"Um, good morning?"

My eyes bulged and mouth opened but no words came out.

"Sweetheart?" My mom's voice came from behind me. "What are you doing here?"

I swiveled around to find my mom coming out of the hallway wearing a silky red robe. She stopped in the kitchen, wearing a concerned expression, and I wanted to yell at her to cover herself up in front of Bernie. "What is going on? Why is Bernie here? Why are you wearing a sexy robe?"

And as soon as I asked the question, the answer was so obvious.

My mouth fell open. "Are you two *together*?"

"What happened to you, sweetheart?" Her eyes trailed down my wrinkled outfit from yesterday, and I realized I hadn't done my make-up or brushed my hair or teeth before I'd rushed out the door.

"I'm looking for Nate." My gaze darted from Bernie to my mom, then I couldn't take it anymore. I darted to the hallway bathroom, grabbed a spare toothbrush from the drawer, and started brushing my teeth *hard*, as if I could scrub away the image of Bernie and my mom in their robes together. In the back of my mind, I rationalized that they were both consenting adults, but *blech.*

I so didn't want to picture my mom that way. Or Bernie, for that matter.

As I brushed my teeth, I readjusted my hair in its twist so I didn't look so disheveled. Moments later, my mom came into the bathroom holding a piece of paper. "I'm sorry you had to find out about Bernie and me this way. But believe me, our relationship is a good thing and should've happened years ago."

I spit into the sink. I rinsed my mouth out with water, then dabbed my face with an ivory hand towel. "How do you figure?"

She leaned against the edge of the sink's countertop. "Bernie and I have had feelings for each other for years. We just never admitted them. We were such good friends, and besides, I hadn't been ready to let your father go."

I let out a breath. "And now?"

"Making the ceramic hot air balloons and painting

them was a way for me to keep your dad close. But subconsciously I now realize painting had also been about finding myself again. I'd stopped working artistically when I married your dad and had you, because there wasn't time for anything else."

I remembered all of the boxes in the foyer. "Are you getting rid of the ceramic hot air balloons? I saw boxes stacked in the entryway . . ."

"I'm sending them to art galleries." She smiled proudly, then held a piece of paper toward me. "Maybe it will make more sense once you read your dad's letter to me."

I took the letter in my hands, then looked down at the familiar handwriting. My letter had been an amazing gift to me, and every time I read it I could almost hear his voice again. The same happened now as I read:

My darling Elizabeth,

If you're reading this, then that means I've gone to wherever the universe has planned for me next. Thank you, my love, for sharing your years with me. You filled my days with much joy and gave me my other greatest love, our daughter.

Knowing you as well as I do, I worry that you'll see my passing on as something sad. But we're only allowed a limited number of years on the earth and I lived mine well, so please be happy for me. If you'll do me the honor of playing one last game, I've made you a Carpe Diem list:

1) Have my ashes sprinkled over the Sierras.

2) Share your art with the world.

3) Fix your biggest regret.

4) Fall in love again.

It's my hope that this list will help you jump-start a new chapter in your life, which I'm sure will be as amazing as the chapters we spent together. I've left a Carpe Diem list for Melinda as well, so please don't give her the insurance money until she's completed each task.

My one last request is for you to walk Melinda down the aisle for me. When you do, tell her how beautiful she is and how much her daddy loves her. Then shake the hand of the man who won her heart, tell him to take care of my girl, and that I'll be looking down on them with love.

When you think of me, always smile. I'm grateful to have shared my life with you.

Love,

Ed

"Oh, Mom . . ." My eyes watered, then I lifted my lashes. "Dad wanted you to fall in love again, and of course I do, too. I was just . . . surprised. That's all." Shocked would be more like it, actually. "I love Bernie, and I'm happy for you both."

She smiled back at me. "Thank you."

My throat tightened as I reread the letter. When I got to the part about my dad's request that my mom walk me down the aisle, I immediately envisioned myself gliding down the white lacy runner with my mom, approaching the tuxedo-clad groom who was smiling back at me with his jade-green gaze.

Then something else happened. As I imagined my mom placing my hand in Nate's, my veil-tinted gaze shot to the translucent man standing beside us. My dad! His worried stare shot through me as his gaze flicked back and forth between and Nate and me. His brows rose as if asking what I was doing.

My gaze lifted, and I stared at my mom. "Where's Nate? He told me he'd be here picking up Dad's ashes . . ."

My mom tilted her head as if confused. "He left to sprinkle your dad's ashes over the Sierras from a hot air balloon."

My heart rate kicked up. "Yeah, but he hasn't driven off yet. His motorcycle is in the driveway . . ."

"He took Bernie's car."

I grabbed the sides of my head. "What? When did he leave?"

"Just before you arrived. Did you change your mind about going?"

"Yes!" Tears blurred my vision, which felt like all too common of a recurrence this week. "And he's not answering his cell phone. Do you know the address of where he's going?"

"I do." She darted down the hall, then came back with a scribbled-on sticky note. "They're launching from here. But I'm afraid he said they were going to take off immediately after he arrives. Something about morning winds being calmer . . . "

Bernie popped his head around the corner from the hall. "Everything all right, ladies?"

No, everything was most definitely not all right. The man I loved was moving to Peru because I'd told him to, and I'd missed my last chance to take a hot air balloon ride with my dad.

"I have to go!" I may have sounded crazy, but I didn't care. I gave my mom and Bernie each a quick hug, then I raced out the door. I backed out onto the street as fast as I could, then put my car in drive and stomped on the gas pedal.

I'd let fear rule my life for too long. From now on, I would seize each day like my dad had taught me. I just hoped I'd get to Nate before he took my dad up for his last flight.

****

I merged into the fast lane and sped down the freeway toward the Sierra foothills, my heart racing. Every time I dialed Nate's cell number the call went straight to voicemail, making me want to throw my phone. I'd been such a coward about sprinkling my dad's ashes from the hot air balloon. This was one of my dad's final wishes and I'd left the responsibility up to someone else because I was terrified of heights.

I couldn't help wondering what Nate thought of my cowardice. He had to be one of the bravest people I knew, just like my dad had been, and he never let fear stop him. Not like I had. But I was *done* letting fear rule my life.

I'd wanted to go up in the hot air balloon with my dad so badly, but I'd been afraid of that little possibility of plummeting to my death. Okay, maybe that wasn't so little. It had sadly happened to my dad. But it also wasn't so likely and my dad had known that when he'd taken the risk. And by skipping chances to do what excited me, I'd been missing the joy those adventures could bring me, especially in a relationship that left me breathless.

I loved Nate. And I'd let him go because he'd considered a trip that of course he would find amazing? That was insane. I could fly to Peru to visit him for the next six months, or however long the job lasted. No, that hadn't been the real reason I'd let him go. I'd been afraid of getting my heart broken again. But we all made mistakes sometimes. Hadn't I just made a terrible one by breaking up with Nate?

My eyes flicked to the clock as I exited the freeway. What were the chances they wouldn't have taken off already? Slim to none. I had to go faster. I slowed to make a right turn, then sped toward the address my mom had given me, imagining the hot air balloon rising above me by the time I arrived, too high, too out of reach. The tension in my body ratcheted up a notch.

Then I spotted the address on a wooden sign ahead of me. I turned down the driveway that led to a dirt parking lot and screeched my car to a halt next to Bernie's sedan. I jumped out of the car, gaze darting around quickly until I spotted an open field. A bright yellow and red balloon lay deflated on its side next to a brown wicker basket. Two male figures stood beside it, and relief flowed through me.

I raced in their direction.

Nate glanced up as I ran toward him at full speed. A look of confusion crossed his face and he moved away from the basket, coming toward me. He wore jeans and a short-sleeved shirt that stretched across his chest in a very appealing way. I stopped seconds before crashing into that hard chest and then fought to catch my breath.

"You didn't go up yet. Right?" I managed to get out between gasps for breath.

"No." He started to reach toward me as if reflexively, but then he looped his thumbs into his back pockets. "Are you here to ride with us?"

"Yes." I nodded, my heart pounding in my ears. "Well, that's one of the reasons I'm here."

A line formed between his brows. "What's the other reason? Is everything all right?"

"No!" My voice echoed through the small valley, and I realized I'd probably spoken too loudly. But, whatever. "This probably won't come out the way it should, but I have something I need to tell you."

His green eyes peered into mine. "What is it?"

"First, I'm not going to take that customer service position at my old company. I'm going to start my own bakery."

"What about Bernie's Bakery? I thought you loved it."

Pain washed through me at the mention of Bernie's

Bakery. The loss felt as real as losing family, but I knew I'd done the right thing by putting Bernie first. An offer of twenty-perfect above asking price was huge, and would help him be financially secure in his retirement. "I'm going to have to let that go, then focus on a second chance. Somehow."

He tilted his head, and gave me a side-glance. "You know my dad turned down the buyer's offer. Right?"

My eyes nearly popped out of my head. "What?!"

"Someone told him you were interested in buying the bakery. And before you say anything, it wasn't me."

"But, who would . . .?" My voice trailed off, but then the image of Bernie standing in my mom's kitchen in his bathrobe appeared in his mind. "My mom." I glanced at Nate, and his expression told me he thought the same thing. "Did you know about them?"

His gaze met mine. "I dropped by my dad's yesterday to check on him. Let's just say it was an inopportune moment for me to arrive unexpectedly."

I shuddered, then confessed, "I saw them in their robes this morning."

"Their relationship is definitely going to take some

getting used to." He blew out a breath, shaking his head. Then he placed a hand on my arm. "But the important thing is that he's selling the bakery to you."

Warmth infused my chest and I felt like my heart was rising as if it were a hot air balloon. I hadn't wanted Bernie to sacrifice the higher offer for me, but it looked like I didn't have a choice anymore. Ironically he was doing what was in my best interest, which was what I'd been trying to do for him. Because of him, one of my dreams was going to come true. Now it was up to me to make my other dream a reality.

"I love you, Nate," I blurted, and my cheeks immediately heated. I couldn't believe I'd just confessed my feelings to Nate in the middle of a dry empty field that smelled suspiciously like cow manure. So *not* romantic. "I know you're going to Peru, but if you give me a second chance maybe I can come visit you? We can ride horses up the Inca Trail, or something."

The corners of his mouth twitched. "You want to ride on the Inca Trail?"

"I might," I said, even though the actual idea of dust and sweat didn't seem as romantically appealing as it had been in my dream. "Look, you are this amazing, adventurous guy, and I'm probably the least risk-taking person out there." I thrust my hands to my chest. "But that doesn't mean we don't belong together."

Now the corners of his mouth curved upward. "Oh, really?"

"Yes!" My mouth puckered, wondering what he thought was so funny. "I'm glad you took that job in Peru, because that's important to you. But I want us to stay together. I want to seize life and live, or whatever. I'm just not sure how to start and . . . are you laughing at me?"

"Maybe a little." He chuckled. "But only because I already turned down the project in Peru."

My tummy fluttered. "You did? But I thought that was the perfect job for you . . ."

"At one point in my life it would have been, but now I'm ready for a new adventure." He slipped his hands around my waist and pulled me close to him. "With you."

Shivers raced down my spine, and I peered up at him shyly. "Even though I'm boring?"

"You aren't even close to boring." He brushed his

fingers along my jawline, studying my face as if taking me all in. Then he inhaled deeply as if savoring the moment. "I love you, princess. Always have, and always will."

Then he pressed his lips to mine, sending tingles throughout my body, along with that lovely feeling of déjà vu that I had the strong suspicion would never end.

****

Taking off in the hot air balloon was more than a little scary. There wasn't exactly a lot of room in this four-person wicker basket and the red fuel tanks took up a lot of leg space. Plus, the burner was pretty loud and the large flame startled me at first. But, I was facing my fears and that was huge.

Now that we'd reached our desired height, everything was quiet as we floated along, and I began to see why my dad enjoyed going up so much. Then I peeked over the rim of the basket, peering at the ground far below, and my stomach dropped. I squeezed my eyes shut. The earth was a *long* way down. Then I felt arms slip around my waist, my back being pressed against a warm, solid chest. Nate.

Once I was comfortable again, I stepped away from him and peered over the edge again on my own. Still scary, but not quite as bad this time. I closed my eyes, enjoying the light wind against my face and letting tranquility wash over me.

When I opened my eyes again, my view had shifted, as if I'd shrunk much shorter. Then my gaze dropped to my hand, which was smaller, and my fingernails glittered with the blue polish that had been all the rage the summer before my freshman year of high school.

A man's familiar hand wrapped firmly around mine, and warmth flooded through my chest. When I lifted my gaze, my dad was looking back at me. He smiled, the sides of his blue eyes crinkling, and he squeezed my hand.

"Daddy," I whispered. Every cell in my body came alive and a small sound escaped me as I gaped gratefully into my dad's eyes, unable to believe he was here with me. He held my gaze, his eyes sparkling as if he'd been waiting for this moment as long as I had. My vision blurred and hot wetness seeped down my cheeks, but the corners of my mouth turned upward.

His eyes drifted to my smile and an expression of calmness spread across his features—a look that could only be described as pure peace. Then he turned his head, staring off into the distance. My gaze followed his and I saw beauty all around me. White clouds. Blue sky. Scattered green and brown land below.

Instead of being scared this time, I felt exhilarated . . . *filled* with all of the joy of truly living. I closed my eyes, breathing it all in. Then something shifted.

My eyes popped open and I glanced down at my French-manicured hand, which was now empty. I glanced up, but my dad was gone. Remembering the words in my dad's letter, I searched the sky frantically. On the highest point, my gaze came to rest where the sky was brightest blue, and rush of familiar warmth flooded through me.

"I love you, Daddy," I whispered, then turned around, taking the cloth bag Nate held toward me. I hugged the bag against my chest one last time. Then I opened the top, held the bag over the rim, and turned it upside down. I watched what almost looked like fairy dust drift away, caught in the gentle currents of the wind, until the contents were gone.

I set the empty bag on the floor then leaned against the rim, gazing wistfully at the ashes dancing in the sky. An invisible heavy cord snapped free inside me, pulling a heavy weight off my shoulders, leaving behind a weightless freedom.

Nate's arms slipped around me from behind, his forearms leaning onto the rim of the basket as he pulled me close and rested his cheek against mine. He didn't say anything to me, and he didn't need to as I nuzzled into him.

I glanced around me to find the ashes, but they now blended with the sky. My dad's love flowed through me and I let go of yesterday, ready to seize all life had to offer me today.

Epilogue

Six weeks later. . . .

I pushed open the yellow shabby-chic door of Bernie's Bakery, *my* bakery, and the familiar *ding-a-ling* of the bell chimed overhead. I couldn't believe I'd left my mom and Bernie's engagement gift in the storage compartment on Nate's motorcycle. Then again, I still couldn't believe I'd ridden on his motorcycle while wearing a silver-sequined cocktail dress.

I'd worn my hair up, showing off the purple streak in my hair, but to say it was mussed from the not-so-elegant motorcycle helmet would be putting it mildly. But, eh. Who cared about looking perfect, anyway?

"I still can't believe my mom and Bernie are getting married." I turned to Nate as we hiked up the stairs that led to the private rooftop terrace. "Won't that make us step-brother and step-sister?"

Nate shuddered, placing his hand on the small of my back. "Let's not think about that."

"Good idea." I chuckled as we arrived at the top of the stairs. But instead of giving my mom and Bernie their gift right away, I tugged Nate over to the railing and glanced around the terrace at my dinner party, which was starting to wind down.

Instead of a girls' night, this time I'd invited couples and friends alike to celebrate my new business. Avery, Mary Ann, Ginger, and even Sarah were here. Ellen and her husband Henry had come too, and this was their first night out since their baby, Henry Holbrook the fourth, had been born. I'd invited my friend Chris from my old job and he'd brought his girlfriend, Gina, with him. The two were such a great couple, I had a feeling they'd be getting engaged soon.

Under the dark evening sky, lights twinkled across the terrace that Ginger had redesigned for me. She refused to let me pay her for her time, which I supposed was a huge perk of having a decorator as a roommate. Even though I could afford my own place now, Fudge was so happy living with Ginger's cats, Gilligan and The Professor, that I didn't want to move and make my pup sad. In truth, I didn't want to move either.

Nate wrapped his arms around my waist, hugging me. I pivoted on my silver heels, twisting away from the party until I was facing Nate. My gaze locked with those jade-green eyes that always took my breath away.

I slinked my arms around his neck, making a humming sound. "Wow."

He rested his forehead against mine. "What?"

I laced my fingers through the soft hair at the back of his neck. "Never thought I could feel this happy."

His mouth curved upward. "I bet I can make you happier."

"How?" I asked, wondering how I could possibly feel any happier than at this exact moment.

"You'll see." He reached into the pocket of his slacks and pulled out a small square package covered in wax paper that I recognized very well. "Close your eyes."

I squeezed my eyes shut as the scent of fudge filled the air around me. When I felt a nudge against my lips, I opened my mouth, welcoming the sugary-sweetness of my favorite chocolate marshmallow fudge bar. "You know me so well," I whispered.

Then his mouth captured mine, and I tasted the

greatest sweetness of all.

The End

SUSAN HATLER is a *New York Times* and *USA Today* Bestselling Author, who writes humorous and emotional contemporary romance and young adult novels. Many of Susan's books have been translated into German, Spanish, French, and Italian. A natural optimist, she believes life is amazing, people are fascinating, and imagination is endless. She loves spending time with her characters and hopes you do, too.

You can reach Susan here:

Facebook: facebook.com/authorsusanhatler
Twitter: twitter.com/susanhatler
Website: susanhatler.com
Blog: susanhatler.com/category/susans-blog

Ellen signs up for online dating because lasting love is all about compatibility . . .

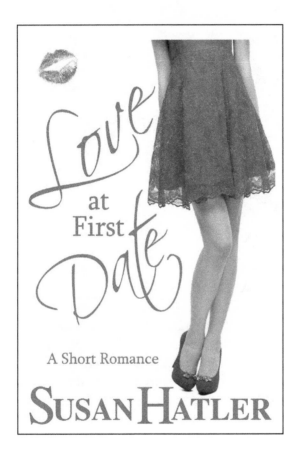

Love
at
First
Date

A Short Romance

SUSAN HATLER

. . . so why can't she stop
thinking about Henry when he's
the opposite of everything she wants?

Truth or Dare is all fun and games . . .

Truth or Date

A Short Romance

SUSAN HATLER

. . . until a spontaneous dare has Gina
falling for the office playboy.

It's Valentine's Day and Rachel can stay home and watch
TV . . .

My *Last*
Blind
Date

A Short Romance

SUSAN HATLER

. . . or risk another dating disaster
by trying yet again for love.

Kristen swears off men, but temptation
swoops in . . .

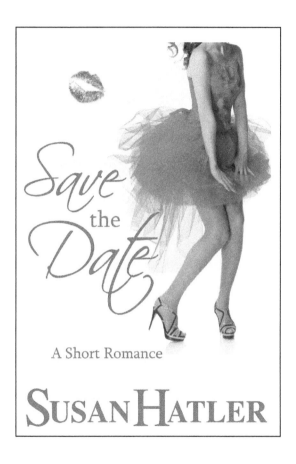

Save
the
Date

A Short Romance

SUSAN HATLER

. . . when her sexy friend Ethan
starts flirting with her.

Will Melanie have to follow her
best friend's narrow dating rules . . .

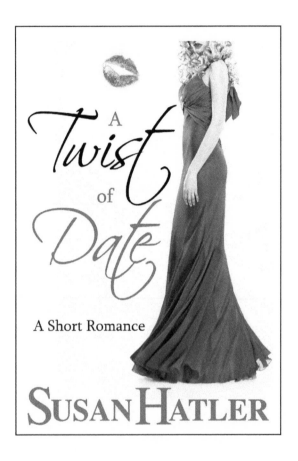

A
Twist
of
Date

A Short Romance

SUSAN HATLER

. . . in order to find lasting love?

Kaitlin agrees to five dates in five days . . .

A Short Romance

SUSAN HATLER

. . . only to fall for the mysterious bartender
who's there to witness them all.

When Jill's promotion is nabbed by nepotism, she
is offered another position on the partner-track . . .

Driven
to
Date

A *Special* Edition

SUSAN HATLER

. . . by pretending to date Ryan—
the man who got her job.

Ginger donates her decorating services
to a charity auction . . .

Up
to
Date

A Short Romance

SUSAN HATLER

. . . and now must work for the one man
with the power to break her heart.

Holly may be living in her dream location,

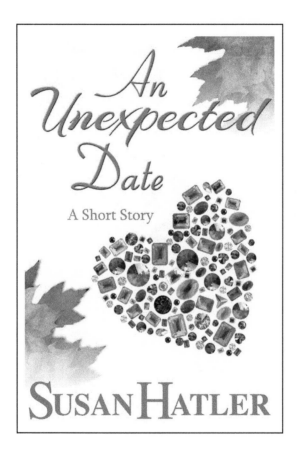

but is her little resort town too small
to attract the right man?

In high school, it's tough enough reading Steinbeck and
Shakespeare . . .

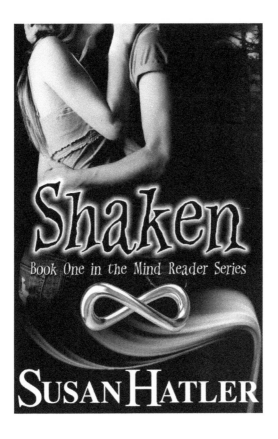

. . . now Kylie has to read minds.